SAP'S WAR

ISBN: 978-0-9684591-7-1

Proofread by Linda Matassa;
all errors are the author's own.

SAP'S WAR

WARD MCBURNEY

To Shelley Lynn Wall
who made it all possible.

It is possible, possible, possible. It must
Be possible.
—Wallace Stevens

Twin pylons rise on Vimy's war-scarred hill,
  Remote, austere, sublime against the sky,
  Telling of victory won, and courage high,
Courage that Death might end, but could not kill.

"War to end war!" — Ah! Bitter, haunting phrase!
  Lie that piled high the holocaust of youth!
  Words spawned in same, by men devoid of truth,
Seeking their ends by dark and devious ways.

Stars shine, birds sing, the little flowers unfold,
  The seasons run their old appointed way,
  Yet still we wait the dawning of that day
For which they died, who now lie stark and cold.

G.R.L. Potter
From *The Epic of Vimy*
(The story of the 1936 Pilgrimage)

I shall never live to like
  the broad ways of the breeze
that kicked our aprons as we hiked
  through avenues of trees —

those vistas of the riot night,
  when sound began to cease
bearing us within its great
  inanimate increase —

'til each Polyphemic roar,
  war-blended to beyond,
stoned us into silence, or
  merely ended sound.

Recording how you blew us clear —
  O Sister wind, surcease;
aid us now in how to sear
  the sights you bore in peace.

   Jennabeth Gray, nursing sister
   Canadian Expeditionary Force

I

WHAT TOOK YOU

"WHAT TOOK YOU SO LONG?" Sapphira asks, standing in that brick-red coat of hers, in the dark, in the cold. Not just any winter, standing anywhere: it's Toronto, and winter is the Winter of 1917–1918—one of the longest, coal-short succession of snaps this already frozen city will ever know—the fourth winter of the war. Which is also (I want to say) but will have to wait, until this slender, shaking other speaks up.

"I had to wait until they were all asleep, and then," she's chattering now, behind those little-rim glasses of hers, but Sapphira has already forgiven her, can only feel (besides the sharp vice of night, which she hardly feels at all, she is so hot with topgallant desire) forgiveness for her friend, the only one crazy enough to join her, on this fool's errand.

"We have to lift it," Sap abrupts—whatever Alley had to add. She can be high-handed with Alley-Who—who worships her, she knows it, all the way from Walnut to Sullivan streets, where each girl, respectively, lives. Alley-Who because she will not tell her name, her full one, even to Sapphira.

"Alhambra?"

"Nope."

"Almeida?"

"Nope."

"Almanacky del Tabacky on the Rhine?"

"Nope."

But there is no time for their guessing game tonight, the one they play, otherwise, almost every time they see each other—usually right off the bat.

"I brought an iron," Alley says matter-of-factly, producing an oh-my-goodness poker from her long, green coat. Still warm with me, she thinks, handing it to Sap, who eyes it like an unwanted chaperone, until Alley says, "Here's how you pry it," and sets her wiry strength to work.

The immense stopper of a sewer cover makes its gaping uh-thud, grate scraping over rim, mouthing under-mother in the dull tang of snow. Sapphira hesitates, looks down; looks up: the face of her friend, focused in the moonlight. Alley will follow her down, she knows, but ought not (something wiped out here, in Sapphira's slate brain) come back up with her—that is, on the other side. Sap doesn't want her there, in the killing yard, or whatever the hell it is she's delving for. Wherever pigs go when they die.

"Who showed you that?"

"John Odd, Junior."

"You didn't tell me you talked to him."

"I had to, when it became clear," she says, eyeing Sap directly with that I-may-not-be-as-pretty-or-poetic-but-smarter-(*definitely*-smarter)-than-you look she has, "you didn't know anything more about underground sewers than you do about abattoirs."

You're just saying that because it's in French, Sap thinks. French for killing. Kiss me, kill me; miss me, thrill me.

"I know enough."

"To get yourself killed."

"I know enough."

"I'm going with you."

It is here, as the girls get ready to descend, that I get to tell you what I wanted to, above. You know that the war is the Great War, the war for civilization, the War of 1914. What's harder to imagine is the not knowing.

When it will end, for instance. Or that already its beginning seems as buried as the creek that Sap and Alley want to access, via this sunken grate, cratered in the ditch before the old fort. Garrison Creek, vaulted under brick, turned under earth, gone. Alive. And Toronto is Toronto in the deep freeze of fate, Imperial outpost seconded to industrial magnates, supplying pork and shells by the boatload overseas. And men. Sapphira's brother, for one. Stan.

2

GASLAND

SHE KNOWS HE IS GONE by the empty body-pocket of
bedclothes beside her. Sister, can you spare a soldier? He's
out there, she thinks, wandering for his front line — the
thing that had sliced them to ribbons, depending on how
close they got to it, and on which side of it they found
themselves — trying to reach, maintain, or trip back
over it — treading howling headlong home: the invisible,
invincible line. Sometimes, it was like it had never existed;
sometimes, it was like the edge of the world: everything that
reached it went over, and never came back again.

They were back. This was the riskiest of all: an
emphatic return. Not a reunion in Toronto — over the
top, in mind — but over the ocean, in a ship, along with six
thousand other veterans, their wives and children, in the
summer of 1936, to open the Vimy Memorial in France.

Open. The word was like line. There was nothing to
open. Those twin pylons were open already, scarring the
sky — or were they opening them, the pilgrims, as they tore
a great hole in the heavens their hearts? She wasn't sure
where the bodies were, here, or in the air, and everything
else seemed a potential wounder, like the teaspoon she had
found embedded in a boy, packed into the shrapnel that had
burst above his head. Jenny raises hers: cascade of raven hair,
threaded grey. Sister Jenny Gray. Three a.m. Stan has left his
trench watch on the bedside table.

At some point, each night, he goes out — ostensibly to
smoke, which she will not permit, in their room above the

kitchen—in St. Julien, of all places, where the Canadians
first were gassed. Three a.m. and he stands by the roadside,
strikes a match, bends his head above its sudden cusp. St.
Julien had been his idea, to skip England and start their own
pilgrimage where the Canadians had, near Ypres. And she had
agreed, hoping for something other than the sight of his back
in bed, or, worse, his ribbing her over her breath at night—*my
little gas alarm.* He actually calls her that. A fine romance.

A smaller pylon juts just down the street, ringed by young
pines, its single figure fingering the moon: a concrete soldier,
head bowed over the heel of his rifle, growing out of stone.

Apollo?

"Apollo," Jenny says to the room. The god touched
her—or was it the god who saved her? Or was it two gods?
Whatever it was, Apollo was the problem, and the girl
became a tree. The girl became a tree, the soldier became
stone, resting on his laurels, and so there were three: Jenny,
Stan, and the god of the line.

Who needed to be turned into what, saved from whom?
Stan, stone already, returned to soldier? The line, rising
into the dark, made concrete by the ridge? Or was it she,
Jenny—*Daphne*—who had to be barked up, carried back
to Canada in leaves, pressed into their pocketbooks with
poppies and forget-me-nots?

She wasn't keen on memorials. Few nurses were. It wasn't
that they didn't get the point, but the sisters knew—in
a way peculiar to them, midway between slaughter and
doctor—how malleable the subjects of these stones had
been. To come upon the statue of a soldier was akin to
finding a petrified fetus in a delivery ward—they weren't
anyone's babies. It rather seemed they'd been stripped of
birth's basics, ripped backwards in time and then re-presented

to the world—without so much as a slap on their backs to cast the gas from their lungs, and breathe.

So, former C.A.M.C. nursing sister Jennabeth Gray gives Lieutenant Athelstan Allward, formerly in command of 13 Platoon, D Company, 108th (Toronto Typographic) Battalion, a pretty wide berth when it comes to—just about anything. She rolls her eyes away from his watch and her body follows, lapsed in a beauty she cannot see. All there, all the time, and Athelstan, out smoking in gasland.

She does not feel him get back into bed beside her but, come sunrise, when she wakes, he is there, moored in morning sleep. Let him. They both enjoy being away from comforts; each competes with the other for independence. Her turn, now, to go out, alone.

3

BLAZE

Scout Captain John Herald leads Blaze by her
bridle through the woods, along the forest track. The light
goes dappling on her back already dappled; her saddle
shines in the sunspots like wet tobacco. John wasn't in the
cavalry—he never rode at the Front, so it seems natural
to Stan to follow them as two—charge and charger—past
the chatty poplars and scrub pines, the lichen-rough stone
surfacing here and there like shell-encrusted whales.

John is in uniform but not in France: the feather tips
of his hair blow over the Canadian Shield, and Stan has
followed them here, from the fields of Amiens, whence
they have been walking since the war ended. Blaze nuzzles
between Herald's shoulder blades; her massive neck—horn
of moon scudding through green leaves—is close enough
to stroke, but John says, "She doesn't like it when you touch
her; you have to be in front of her to do that. There's a
clearing up ahead; you can touch her there."

Stan looks down, and sees strands of barbed wire wrapped
around her fetlocks, but the horse is whole: no shell, no shard,
no wounds of any kind. "You think you can show me where
you found her? Can you show me the quarter where she came?"

"If there's a storm," John answers, "she'll come from the
sky, then; she comes from the sky, again, when that happens."

He doesn't turn to speak. Stan sees the horizon of his
cheek, his khaki collar, the three red ampersands stitched
above the green battle patch on his shoulder. So. They
finally changed it.

4

FLAVELLA

SPRING, TORONTO, 1917. The city thaws its beams
and wheels. White-hot steam, sweat-black coal; new
engines of misdirection. Slaughter, the houses are full of
slaughter—both here and abroad—most of her sons and all
of one daughter: Sapphira Allward. Sap. She drags the streets
for run-off gutturals—seizes quick, dingy glimpses of herself
in new blue, fading already above her one-act society of waif
and stray, girl and animal, beating upstream, threshing raw
vision from the grainiest way. Swings down lower Niagara,
thick with industry, poverty, and strange-vested men in
rented rooms; sweeps past the coffin factory, its belts and
flywheels humming with toil; peeps past bay windows and
sees settees gone to seed, pianos broken up for firewood,
parlour-papered walls curling at the corners—a slow-
match city, pitching towards fire. Busied in details: hand-
filled factories swollen with want, hand-empty households
collapsing into must; blocked-in parlours like organ stops,
pounding forte poverty, the imprecations of in-bricked lives:
fear, abuses, tendernesses never known. Abattoirs, dye works,
the chuff-and-unt of steam freight. Sheds and storage sheds
for these; throughways and alleyways bouncing with light.

And then, she saw the refuse, move. No. Snout! In, out!
A pink, dark-with-soot, piglet. Pig … let … out. Pig-let-me
(touch) you. She gives something between a snort and a
sniff; her four legs jerk together—a footstool, kicked with
recognition. Pig-let-me. Touch you. Pet pig. Mitt-less hand,
witless heart, frightened snout. Pet, pet. My pet. Piglet.

She followed her home, of course—which was fine, at first;
Flavella (her father, Fred Allward, had called her, *Your fellah*,
even though she was a girl pig) was small enough to pass as
a pet—even in cash-strapped, ashen-eyed Toronto—in the
bold spring of 1917. Victories—real ones: Vimy Ridge, Hill
70—would bolster confidence. Passchendaele was not yet;
Operation Michael, a winter away; the final Hundred Days,
unthinkable. Toronto rode the high before the low before
the wild finish of the war, and the pink rump of Flavella,
rooting every back yard on the north side of Sullivan Street,
was seen as just one more eccentricity from that strange girl,
who skipped school to volunteer at the shell factory canteen,
drew pictures of nothing on the porch with the simpleton
next door, and *typed*—no scrawl for her—*typed* letters to
her officer brother at night.

Gladys, her mother, forbore and, by so bearing, joined
an invisible army of women, faces set, bodies apart and
alone, united in fronting raft upon raft of cold nights
lost to wholesale rage. The ordinary women of Toronto,
with their sober step—75 paces to the minute, was that
it?—stalked past sergeant recruiters parked on street
corners like scythesmen on a lark, swathing the produce
of their entire, empire lives—expecting, not only to pay
nothing upon deceit of the goods but, should their sons
miscarry, expecting death to quit the debt they owed to that
other mother, England, who rendered their last accounts
in clipped.stop.sentences as short as stop.regret. Rather
stopper their mouths, these mad mothers, whose born sons
and younger brothers burn fallow for heaving fields. At sea,
their lives laved under scudding tons of mud. At least, they
were allowed to be proud.

So Gladys Speranza Allward allowed her beautiful—and almost dutiful—daughter, Sapphira, to do whatever the Samson H. Jake she wanted.

She wandered, when hardly anyone did anymore (wartime swallowed the wayward). She did her bit, to make up for it. And she dreamt of a city of brick so newly fired it baked her brains just walking home. She was as old as the century and was of an age and susceptibility that words could stoke like hot rocks. At times, it seemed to some—themselves sleepless, waiting for news or for no news, fumbling for telegrams, received or seen received: this city of insomniacs—some declared they could hear Sap whack and ding her type-written way into dawn.

5

WHACK-AND-DING

Toronto, 1916

DEAREST BROTHER:

Here I am, whack-and-ding, yours faithfully ever, and never on time, with another of a series of instalments (if you can take time off from that dreadful thing they call a war) to witness one of mine.

She was the size of half-a-minute. Nothing if not elliptical. Downright parenthetical. And inimical, well, everyone was—to her. I scouted her from the safe edge of the paly-ground fence (yessir, Mister, that's paly-ground, not play ground miss-whacked). And what will you have, my little Miss Whacked-about?

You'll have me, digging you out with whumps and fists; you'll have me, tearing my hair out (along with that of several others, all stranded together in this war(d) we call Toronto) to get at the roots of you.

Whatsyername? I ask her, all fawned in my rungs of lung-bracketing hands. Alley, she says. Who? I say. Alley. Alley-Who? She won't tell. Well. Now we are two too—much for you, Piperoo. Don't ask me to come explaining. Everything. Again.

Yours ever,
Sap!

6

CARMAN, MANITOBA

CARMAN, MANITOBA kept its Main Street to itself. In an era when Prairie towns were railroaded in or out of existence—the inhabitants rebuilding around the line that took their yields—Carman kept its multicoloured, paned-in verandas and Second Empire mansard roofs right where she wanted them, and bent the rails to serve *her* will, wound around the serpent bends of the river Wye, in a landscape where the sky alone seemed substantial—everything else a chugging, puttering, momentary intrusion. And to Fred Abercrombie, in from Roland with an open wagon to gather supplies, nothing had been so intrusive as the war, which had taken all the local heroes of his youth, strung them up in khaki, and plunged them down the tracks to oblivion. He didn't go. He was—just—too young. Young, and a bit slow: the only son of a man with three farms and a general store to run. When they returned, the ones he had looked up to in his boyhood drank and swore and pissed on the sidewalks—in plain view. He vowed never to touch the stuff, and he never did.

It's hard for us to picture how the country people walked, how they read expressions, how they knew what was what. They stare rigidly out of glass negatives and seem at one with the impossible china sets they brought with them from overseas. Fred was the first of the young men to smile, actually smile at the camera in his Sunday best, those weekends when the Abercrombies gathered to gorge themselves on beef and beans and pie. He was serious, Presbyterian, a big eater, and a good dancer.

He carried his whale of a frame like a sack of feed, hefty, upright, without the slightest regard for his waist or hair or any other line. His favourite phrase at a dance was, Would you like to have a turn on me? (The orchestra set up in empty animal stalls below; they danced aloft to the music through the floorboards.) And if anyone asked him outside after—a girl, I mean, if a girl took his arm and wanted more—Why I'm just fine in here, he'd say, and find another partner. He wasn't afraid of sex or women or the female fact: he was a farmer through and through, and knew the calving came with everything else. He was an elder in the church at the age of 27, a pillar of community, the son of Providence. The simple fact was, the man loved to dance.

7

BACK THEM UP

AN EARLY APRIL wakening, damp Flanders yawning its
beeks and streams. Frost on the ground and, above that, a
mist, over which roofs and tree-tops ride, the land a ghosted
sea. She walks along the road to where the statue props the
dawn, and from the fields surrounding come daughters and
fathers, mothers and boys, some with baskets, others with
tools, and one leading a massive, Belgian horse. She had read
about how they do this, read that the people gathered when
the bowed stone rose up alone. Will Bird. *Thirteen Years
After*. A series of articles for *Maclean's*, collected into one,
thin, aftertaste of a testament. *The Old Front Revisited*.

The statue shouldered above the mist, the mist — she has
to think, *in this place* — like gas, wreathing from cylinders
staunched into the German lines. The circle of young
pines — clipped by gardeners to resemble shells, and the
lower junipers, to evoke shell holes — drown in it.

Jenny takes a deep breath. Something not right still hangs in
the air. But that day, farm animals, civilians, French Algerians,
all came running — rats from the sinking ship of earth — and
the Canadians, pressed behind revetments that wouldn't stop
a bullet, watched and wondered. Neither Stan nor Jenny were
there when it happened — it was already legend by the time
they got to France: how the Canadians held the line, the very
air their enemy, and counter-attacked, bayonets at the end of
their jammed rifles, swinging butts in place of musketry.

She reaches the memorial, and reads through another mist
the only lines that hold, now, in a landscape such as this:

THIS COLUMN MARKS THE
BATTLEFIELD WHERE 18,000
CANADIANS ON THE BRITISH
LEFT WITHSTOOD THE FIRST
GERMAN GAS ATTACKS THE
22–24 APRIL 1915 2,000 FELL
AND LIE BURIED NEARBY

Something about the lack of punctuation, the line breaks as arbitrary as fate, snags her nurse's heart. The final words of the dying. Are they in the mist, too, she wonders, the first to fall? Are these shadowy Belgians their stand-ins? Caps, not helmets, on their dandelion heads; hardly a gun, machine or field, in support. Most did not know war. None knew how to fight without lungs. Not to mention arms: kicking the bolts of their overheated hunting rifles open, breathing through piss-soaked puttees. She takes the visitors' book from its place in the wall, a pencil from the cup kept full and sharp, and writes without thinking, *Back Them Up!* She bangs the book back into its chamber, knocks over the pencils, and does not notice how the farm folk disperse and the mist lifts, until she thinks of Stan.

Making love twenty years after was one thing; making love in France, now, altogether different. He can't. He says. She rolls her eyes, as poppies wink up at her from the margins of the road. She was grateful to have his hands on her again, but just taking her hand at the statue — not this one: the Sons of England statue, after the Corps Reunion concert party in Toronto — was the best thing he ever did for her. He was singing, what, *Sister Susie's Sewing Shirts for Soldiers*? Some damned thing.

Or was it only that he said, with Colonel Leading, Major Stock, and Art Cane standing behind her, "Hullo, sister," took her hand, and kissed her? She should bring him here: putting Stan and stone together is always good for a song. And she, would that she had grown firmer with the years, to be made like him, his ever-young, pulseless Pygmalion, shaped but never softened, his hands forming her from his marble heart.

8

INFANTRY

Then came word to raise the Typos,
drawn from sullen blocks of industry,
hand-picked heralds of the urban dawn,
cased within the city grid. An overseas
battalion of typesetters, released
to make the news they chased, and history
records that they alone of all the troops
of targeted civilians — happy dupes
of sergeants who would tell the moon and stars
that they could serve together in the wars — these
alone retained their fellows in the line,
neither redistributed nor melted down.
Toronto-trained, entrained for Halifax,
thence billowed overseas — so many fulsome sacks,
swung in hammocks strung to be emptied
and bound within the chase of England. These
are all my testament, my lost paternity.
O, open up the hell box and recast
their bold-faced bodies, lest we forget
the plots in which their rows are ever set
in Picardy and Flanders. They saved
the nations of the earth, and giving, gave
all they had at Vimy and the Somme, Lens,
Hill 70, Canal du Nord, Mons,
and other places without name — little
humps of vantage, vales of misery.
I say, this fount of youth, these lowly i's —

invisible, invincible — the skies
bannered with the tramp of their reproof,
imagine these and take my simple words —
death-corrected lines of infantry —
on faith as able witnesses of war
fought to end all wars and set us free.

Stan put the foolscap down, caught his breath. He looked at
his former colonel, the Old Man an old man indeed, now that
87 winters had settled on that snow-white head of his. The
fading light caught the ruff of it as he swivelled in the sun.

"It's a great honour, sir," Stan managed, at last, looking
at pages as foxed as their author's hands. Period paper:
he had kept the cheap, travelling stationery of the 108th
Battalion — an ampersand standing for the numeral eight
(10&th), clustered at the top of each page in a spray of
irregular maple leaves — and was typing the battalion history
on it, in something like heroic couplets.

"Honour! It's a half-baked ass of donkey served to Fritz
with bombs and plonk is what it is, Allward; but I can't
finish it."

Stan looked down.

"Look, Mister, this is for us, and by that *us* I mean the
Battalion, the Toronto Typographic Battalion, the One-O-
Anders, the Typos, the boys. No one else is going to buy
it, let alone read it. You can do whatever — for the love of
lyddite, lieutenant — you can do whatever the theatre of war
crossed with the word is capable of. Besides, you've become
much more than my amanuensis."

Truly. One fine day in 1936 the colonel's daughter,
Constance, was delivered of a baby girl, and her grandfather's
bags and papers had followed, delivered from noise he

could not abide to no fixed address—anywhere without one "Moaning Minnie" wailing up and down the stairs like a klaxon-assed funicular.

"Father—the baby. Don't talk like that." But he had wanted to say something other than an over-inventive oath. He had been, in his time, both father and grandfather to six thousand men: father, in that he had raised them from the typographic tradesmen resident in the city in 1915; grandfather, in that he was (almost) never allowed to lead them, personally, into battle. Instead, he got to act as middleman between the brass hats and the brazen, frozen, liquid muck that passed for terrain overseas. Into that cauldron, moonscape, or morass, he ordered them to go, his helmeted hail-and-hellmet progeny, and watched as each and every one of them slipped—just—past him, heading up the line.

What use, metaphor, when, with signalers, message maps, and forward saps shambled with severed limbs and spattered, what matter what he *thought*, who could not find out a single certain thing, often for hours at a stretch? Secreted in a dugout, his mind raced to piece together a picture of the unguessable already gone, calling in artillery support to co-ordinates stretched tighter than the strap of his Tin Lizzie.

Sunken eyes from a sunken road, he saw them come back, or what was left of them, and could simply no longer abide pain at one remove. This was not his child; they were not his children. Up and down, up and down; the line, the stairs, the god-knows-where; infancy and infantry: crying.

9

AND NO

TRUTH BE TOLD, John Audet Herald entered Carman like a rumour, all painted with tongues. Someone saw him by the way; someone saw him behind a shed; someone saw him leading a horse—a military horse—out on the edge of town. Some saw him in uniform; some in shirtsleeves—with his khaki cap pushed back; some saw the straw blonde of his hair and some his distinctive gait, as he loped over the fields towards the old quarter section where he had worked for Ed Abercrombie before the war. Then, people started to see him in town—*in* Carman. Or, they just missed him.

"That was John Herald who went out."

"What, *now*?"

"Right past you."

"That was *John*? Little John Herald?"

"All six-feet-two of him, looking just like he did before the war."

"Surely not."

"Well, sadder. And wiser. But him—and no mistake."

He even showed up in the beer parlour of one of the two hotels in town, although it always turned out to be the *other* one, drinking a …

"Something he called a panachy at the counter."

"A *what*?"

"*Pan-ah-shay*. It's French. Says they drink it there all the time."

"He told you that?"

"Well, somebody said he did."

"You heard him?"

"Sure I heard him, just as I was going out."

For Fred Abercrombie, to Fred Abercrombie, insofar as Fred Abercrombie was concerned, it didn't happen/seemed queer/wasn't possible. John had worked for Fred's father on the three farms (there was now only the one left, and it was Fred's) that had made Edward Abercrombie a force to be reckoned with in the local-harvest-locust-just-dust of pre-Depression rural Manitoba. Fred didn't talk that way and he had no use for those who did, but there was something of the run-on shell game with this Herald affair. Was he or wasn't he?

Killed, not missing; buried, not inscribed on the Menin Gate or any other paragranite of death untold, folded into manure and sewn into geometric islands that teethed the battlefields of Europe like suckers on glass. Killed, Fred remembered, and remembered her, Mary Helen Degault (pronounced duh-go, with the accent on *go*), collapsing in the kitchen when he came to tell her the news.

John's people, whomever and wherever they were, well, there weren't any. John was technically Ed's number-one hired hand but he just as well could have been his second son. Or first. He was slow and swift; slow, like Fred, but deliberately so. When he had to move—when the threshing was on or the haying underway or an animal broke loose or a seeder broke down or the skies broke open, John moved like quicksilver, moved like thought, and Fred thought he learned from John in those times. Learned that the last shall be first and he had lasted. John went off to war. John left Mary Helen with a lock of hair. John left Mary Helen in Fred Abercrombie's care.

"You look after her," he said, that last afternoon. Fred had done that and more; he saw that she made one of the twelve who taught in the as-many-roomed public and high school, and saw that she kept her class when the market crashed, and no, she would not marry and no, she would not dance and no. No. No.

And down she went the day he died to her. Died on the floor of her kitchen in Roland, in the yellow house next to the road next to the church next to the windbreak next to the news that John was dead. Open prairie. Open like a prayer that never shut. Shout. No. No. No.

Fred remembered, she clung to him almost, her hands curled on his chest as if willing it to be John's, failing, and turning like dry leaves as down she went, a stook undone, the hem of her dress spilling out, whisk whisk, undone. Fred got down on his haunches, and did the only demonstrative thing in his life, to her: he stroked a wisp of hair from her forehead. Stroked and looked and said nothing.

"There, there." Maybe that. And then went for water and a doctor. There was a time of shock, of night wanderings, of sandy-headed moonlight floating over fields. Fred kept his distance, and kept his eye on her, too — he could do that. Sunday afternoons, if she missed the service. And then, one day in 1924, she was off to normal school in Winnipeg, normal school and no fooling. She took Fred's arm in public, she let him lead her to Communion at church, but she would not dance. She was one of those who stayed faithful to her memories. People did that, then. It was an option. No one told them to get on with their lives. They were not afraid of dying.

So, Fred just loved her. Loved her and never married. Not until he was in his forties and she was … gone away. Loved her and never wasted her with childbirth. She baked him pies. They were not in love. Fred loved her. He did.

10

RUNGS

SAP AND ALLEY look down the hole. Not much bigger than
a miracle, Sapphira thinks. Frozen, Alley adds, silently. Each
hears the dim thrum of the other's moth-wings thoughts
beat against the lanternless night. They have one (a storm
lantern), but no idea of how to get it down there, swinging
against their scarves as they descend to—

"How far down is the creek?" Alley asks.

"Fifty paces."

"How do you know?"

Sapphira doesn't answer. She takes out her first surprise,
drawn from the deep pockets of her heavy winter coat. A
torchlight. A battery operated torchlight.

"Gee," Alley says.

"We don't have extra batteries," Sap snaps back. "I want to save
this for later. We've got to get the lantern down there, somehow,
but not lit, is my guess, not lit while we're going down."

She turns on the torch, and shines its eager eye down the
round mouth. Darkness visible. No, something, two rows of
somethings, pronging out from the brickwork.

"Gee," Alley says. She always says that when she's at a loss
for words. It makes her seem like she was twelve, Sap thinks.
I am twelve, Alley answers, in Sap's mind.

"You are not!" Sapphira says, out loud. The girls stare,
then giggle, like lovers on a first discovering.

"What are they, anyway?" Alley asks, looking down at the
long succession of rungs, rust-red in the torch light.

"Horseshoes," Sapphira answers.

II

EASY, GIRL

SHE'S SHIFTING PIES on the counter, slipping barefoot on
the linoleum, lifting cloths from cooling tops (checking,
rechecking; covering, recovering), when she hears the
nicker of a horse outside, and something else, low and
slowly — "Easy, girl" — his voice more a waft of sunlit chaff,
seen through the window. She thinks of his impossible hair,
which she used to bury within her, unearthing suddenly a
hope so wild it nearly splits her where she stands.

"Easy, girl."

Her skin catches fire and freezes at once, she cannot tell,
and is walking to the door as if floating over marble: there is
a horse, and — blessed, blessed, the substitute for swearing
hits her ears like fists in dough — hand, of God, oh God, *that*
hand? Stroking the stairwell of her neck — the horse's — hers
turns as the door-jamb gives way to open Prairie.

"Easy."

His hair beneath that cap. Still, it could be anyone's. Her
hand reaches in front of her, as if she were walking in attic
dark, unsure of furniture. She knows he knows she's there,
standing behind him, shaking now, vision running under
mother-of-pearl, orient jasper, simple tears. The horse gives
a jerky nod. He turns.

And catches her as she swoons, lowers her gently
groundward, where she curls and howls, cursing the dirt,
this blessed pain burning up and down the pillared bending
of her spine.

"Easy, girl. Easy."

When she springs around him like a bear trap even John is taken aback, almost thirty years of clenched-in-death giving way like fencing under floods — the ship is going down, gunwales under hoops of hope and stays, as he lifts her, up he lifts her, smiling, into oceanic eyes.

"Really you?"

"Yes, me. As real as you want me to be."

She pauses on the lip of that for what must have been an eyelid's flutter, enough light to break into the kitchen with a crash, what she knows cannot last, can only be mis-taken.

Hast thou given ... my true love, living ... lost, at last, to me?

12

LIKE SNOW

Starry paste of painted night;
  the door nor red nor green;
yawning under awning light
  of what I've never seen.

Past or future? In its paws,
  and stretched-out in between,
purrs the present, where we pause
  until it's all we've been.

THAT WAS WHAT she wound up with, a budding
metaphysical. Poem. Sapphira. It had taken her a while to
get there. First, it had been in iambic pentameter, to please
Stan — and short: two four-line stanzas (rooms, he'd told
her; think of them as rooms — and so she put two, one
for them, and one for guests). She thought it was good,
and, unhappy as I am to show her sources, I must tell you
that the idea came to her when standing, not in *The* Ward
itself (St. John's Ward, the dark heart of Toronto), but in
front of a painting by Laurel Agnes Starker, hanging in the
unfortunately named Provincial Gallery of Pictographic Art.
  "Difficult to tell," Alley had said, the day that Sap
suggested they go there (anywhere where she would not
be the main attraction, Sap sighed within herself, worn out
with myopic adoration), "difficult to tell," she said, pushing
her eyeglasses up her nose like trip-wire, "whether the first
term is a noun or adjective."

The gallery, housed in an enormous barn of a faux, beaux Greek temple in the Exhibition grounds, had a reputation for the garish, the innovative, and the rigidly conventional—categories only seemingly at odds with one another. Sap took him there, too—John Odd, Junior—when their mothers could spare an afternoon away from worry, wide-eyed and sketchbook-busy. But if Sap thought Alley would swap flesh and blood for canvas and paint, she had another think coming.

Sap took art seriously. Some children, as they become young people, simply do—the same way that anything that you actually touch, and that touches you back, does. So what was the matter with Alley's hand roving behind Sapphira's pinafore? Playing house, playing bed, playing love at night. It's not that Sap didn't like it, and nothing told her it was wrong, because her mother, who would have, had she known, didn't. They both liked Alley very much. What she could not account, or make up, for was the terrific sum of untrustworthy gold that Alley heaped, quite figuratively, at her tiny feet every day.

Where did it come from, that crazy need? And why didn't Sap have it? Of course you have it, Stan said, in the trenches, in her mind, in a letter home. You just have it for something else. You make things. You're a maker, not a wannamaker. He oversaw most of her creativity, whether he was there or not. Actually, he was never there. He was always overseas, when she was old enough to learn, and then she was gone, before he was young enough to teach.

Anyhow, the poem had sprung from paint, as thick as plaster, at one with the houses Starker liked best. She painted in Toronto's old Ward, just as others did, only, she didn't make quick, colour cameos to take to her studio (which she was too poor to afford; she painted in her parlour); she set up an easel in the very streets—Elizabeth, Chestnut, Agnes, Hagerman—and finished her work where it began. Winters, she wore fingerless gloves to the bone; summers, the sun made moth-wings from her parasols. Her subject was colour—the variegated, fading-vivid pastels that haunted the Ward like a second spring.

There was hardly any separation, those days, between the materials of art and life—which is why war was so terrible—but that's another story. Sap carried those bulky pentameters around for a day or two, and then they shed their padding to settle into the spare, rhythmical hymn-form that everyone knew best:

> *Love Divine, all loves excelling,*
> *joy of heaven, to earth come down;*

What it came down to was a cutting away—or was it, rather, a sparer form, carrying itself closer to the body, like the old drill books said? Nothing quaint about that, when you consider what use Frederick the Great had made of them—his Prussian automata—men, made toys, loading and levelling their muskets—was it possible?—*six times a minute.* The first mechanical army, moving on a single spring.

It's winter in most of Starker's paintings, which merely serves to bring the colours out of their cloth pockets and into her hands—Sap's for streets and Alley's for Sap and all for the untouchable *tout partout* of art.

She was just starting out; what we call allegory was as available to her as hopscotch: *the door nor red nor green.* Did she look beyond—as we say—beyond the two coats, each an epitome of the other (that is, the actual door an epitome for the painting, the painting an epitome for the door, and both aping the dye in their respective overcoats), and cast off both for the nakedness Alley sought?

Probably. We'll never know. It hardly matters—or mattered, to Sapphira, that is. No one had to tell her that awning yawning under light could not be cased in punctuation, that each word meant most left entirely to its own devices—which were, precisely, the words on either side of it, and through them to all the words that are.

Love short-circuits art, Stan added, but Sap knew he was being an ass. "Stop being an ass," she said. "Or, if you can't help it, have another head, instead of none—like that two-headed donkey your machine-gunner keeps going on about."

What was Mister Double-Butt doing in Sapphira's poetry? Absolutely nothing. She was merely trying to be everywhere, and Alley, to be here, where Sap was, composing at the kitchen table, the frozen city thawing in her mind and the actual purr of Mister Halliday, their old cat, rising and falling in her lap like beggar's yeast.

"Let me read you what I wrote."

"It's getting late; I'd better get going."

"You walnut. I meant, read it to you in my room."

"Liar."

"Okay-I'm-going-bye!"

"Wait!"

And so they scrambled up, two stanzas, four hands, two girls, and as many arms and legs, climbing the stairwell and falling into Sap's room like snow.

13

LET HER

DEAR ME:

Let her kiss you! Everywhere. Let her, there and there and
there! Don't be unforward, sun brother. Be clear. Of fear.
And let her, let her, let her.

This is a let-her letter; they don't censor the ones coming
to you, do they? Nor yours neither, I don't think. My friend
Alhambra (I really do have a friend named that, and she
really does call herself Ham), she has a brother who's a
Private Soldier in the Twentieth Battalion and she says his
letters come to her with all these little bits cut out, like a
Christmas ornament only nobody hangs it up or makes
them happy about it.

Miss-the-Spinster Hawkingthorpe saw Flavella in her
garden the other day and said someone should make a meal
out of her. I said I'd b- f----- i- I d----t m--- a m--- out of her
f------ l----- b---- of a dog. *That* shut her up. But I self-censor.

They're here, you know, although, not back yet, is my
guess. Will they ever be? I wonder. And I won't say they look
at me funny because they don't and it's easy to talk with
them because hardly anyone else does I just start in on my
way home.

So hey Mister, hey Mister what happened to your leg
and he it got chopped off looking for eggs and me they
must have been big ones and he they were loaded and me
with some big looking chicks he that exploded; Mister, hey
Mister, what took your eyes and he why from looking too

long at the sky and me it must have been really bright and he so much so it all became night and me can you see me by feeling me here try my face and that's all right Sister this ain't the right place; and Mister, hey Mister, what's wrong with you and he I came back just to see who sent me to ... to become this way and me what way is that and he stood up or tried but fell right there on the walk. Thank goodness it was still a wooden one.

He said, "That's all right, little Miss; since I got back nothing of me works so good."

So you see I've been busy. Let Jenny make much of you, Athelstan—I suddenly feel so old telling you that. Maybe the war grows us faster at home, too.

Got to go and appear repentant next door; don't repent too much (or at all, Stanson—take my word for it, just *don't*) over there.

Yours ever,
Sapphira

14

RABBIT, RUN

BILL OSTIC peered through the glass darkly, and the first thing he saw was a face, his face, with the dusky fields of Ypres passing through his eyes. The reconstructed windmill brushed his nose, a pale white road ran out his mouth, as if it were a tongue and he, a vast skull—a one-man Menin Gate in bone—through which they went, still, up the line—his memories, woken in this rented bus, taking them, quite literally, over hell's half-acre.

Well, more than that. How many acres of reclaimed soil? How many lives claimed trying to calm it down, flatten it out, fattened with corpses and ripe for the richest harvests Belgium had ever known? The ground at Waterloo, he'd read, had been spongy underfoot for years after. And he'd already dreamt of walking these fields like an enormous box spring, the spring in his step the winter of the world.

But the land, the land, reconstituting itself where it grew—how could that change not change you—its spring for your fall? And so, sardonic Bill had signed up for the Vimy Pilgrimage out of something like hope, which he kept nestled against his tobacco-lined chest—a wounded animal, something that might, if mishandled, tear the living guts right out of him. He could set it free, maybe, over there. Here. They were here, now; it was night, and they were as lost as a two-assed donkey looking for the Front.

Naked under about a stone's weight of auburn hair, a woman flowed in the seat next to him. She turned her baleful, shining eyes towards his. "Millions now return to the Front," she said. "Just don't part your hair down the back." A jolt, and the corporal's face bumped against the window he had almost dozed right through. She was gone. Typical.

The bus stopped and Bill got out to piss. Art was arguing with the driver over how to get to Vancouver Corner. Hit or miss. Bill struck a match, threw the devil away. Lighting nothing. What friction had they left behind, that they should find it, here, matchsticks to stop a whale? And how on God's fusty earth could they hoop that into future hope?

Words were crazy-making. There are no war words.

He had started reading, nevertheless. Stan tutored him, evenings at the Toronto Armouries, after square-bashing. Out of Allward's haversack came Victorian tomes end-papered open.

"Don't think of these as literature, Mate," Stan said. "They're manuals. Of exercises. *How to Reassemble the Lewis gun that lost the Battle of Eden,* in twelve easy steps. Instructions. *The Tactical Employment of Despair.* There are a lot of books with that as a subtitle. Or this one, by that Russian: *How to Kill Old Women at a Profit.* Just make that assumption. Don't talk too much about things that cannot be seen." (He'd lifted that last from the *Method of Instruction in the Lewis Gun;* Bill knew it.)

That cannot be seen. Like that woman, under her hair. He turned back to the bus, and a hare — peripheral — sprung in front of him — phantom — dashing through the headlights: flashed back into the fields. The night was alive with them, and they were all, running.

15

CHARLIE'S

GRATEFUL FOR THE HUBBUB, Allward sealed his mind. Where was he? In Charlie's on Queen, in a booth at the back. His feet stirred unswept leavings beneath the table, but he did not look down. Uncertain ground. Hadn't that been war's first lesson? It might give way. At any time of day. In winter, the men became entrenched within their clothes — officers had to shout to cut them loose, get them to disrobe, scrub themselves clean. It was as if they, the soldiers, felt the ground reform around them, in the mud that clung to every stitch of them like burs from the fields they would never walk as boys again. Let what will stick to them — and what stuck with them could at least be counted on to not give way, undermined, mole-eaten. Blown sky-high like the moonglow of their covered skin.

The whole city was like that to Stan, in the years after the war, but particularly the 1930s, when everything stopped growing, changing, and swift became sifted-with and very, very dirty. You can still find soot-dark brick in Toronto, out back of the soaring façades at King and Yonge — the very matrix of change, heart of the city — and to see these old façade backs in blackface was like coming upon coloured men in the Canadian Corps. Oh, are *you guys* here? Nova Scotians from Africville, their thin, red line ravelling all the way to King George's army in the war against the colonies, Black Spartans relegated to hauling salvage.

Stan had seen them in the back areas, and knew Sir Sam would have had them fight in the front lines. And he took the same comfort, in France, from men with that much past, that he did, later, from the coat-dusted brick of post-war Toronto, or the soldiers of his platoon from the earth that gloved them in stiffens of dun, the teeming jubilee that each cast off, at last, before the scalding, freezing, nakedness of war.

Given that, what was to be done about Jenny, undone in his arms? Oh, arms and the man! Arms and men and war and war's alarms — it was all one to her. He'd rather be sealed in his mind, sealed in his city, sealed in his uniform, revealed only in his terms. Which were not forthcoming. And so. Night after night, after they were, at last — I was going to say, remarried, but in fact, rather than truth — married, he lay beside a still and very epitome of whatever his lost lust had sought, and felt, nothing. She was not his terms. No kidding.

And so they both longed for France to interpose its foreign tongue between the teeth of their predicament, standing on a ceremony that could not make them young again, but that might at least let them sit down together and eat.

16

PADDING

BEING CONFINED below decks made it all that much easier, although one paid the price of forgoing fresh air. Margaret Macdonald, but recently made Matron-in-Chief of the Canadian Army Medical Corps' nurses overseas, had the canny notion of clearing the decks for just that reason.

Was she remembering her own, first voyage, athwart the Atlantic to reach the South African War? Surely not that far. Forward, I mean, nowhere near as forward as these couples were on the *Franconia*. At night, the bulkheads were simply padded with them, and Margaret was the last one to want to flush them out.

It was her first, great show of trust in her sisters — that they would take the injunction to remain below, at night, for precisely what it was: a curtsey, on the one hand, to military authority and the mores with which they had been raised, and a bow, on the other, to desire. That, and she would not prowl the decks at night — like a vole in heat, she joked to herself — in order to discover ... what, exactly? That her nurses knew how to keep misconception at bay? A baby meant no more nursing for you, Lieutenant Miss, and no mistake.

It was the fall of 1914, and they were on the odyssey of their lives, and not only theirs, but the generations of women proceeding them who had never been shipped overseas, as officers — officers in a major (and Macdonald actually was one), modern war requiring female (making her the highest ranking woman in the world) care.

That got out of the way, what, exactly, could happen?

Romance? Good! They were going to need the distraction, on their half-days off, their occasional leaves. Sexual release? On a boat bursting with animal and human *vir*, the odd shudder could be counted as a positive boon. Otherwise the men were liable to come to blows in the corridors. Not over women — over nothing — and nothing was precisely what Macdonald was going to report on disembarking in England. Nothing unbecoming an officer or an officer and a lady occurred beyond the squeeze of an arm at the day railing, a blush after swelling seas slammed two future pen pals together in the course of their shipboard duties.

Of which there were plenty — the Major saw to that. Lectures on military nursing, and the military in general. Drill. Physical "jerks." Macdonald knew enough to guess the nature and gravity of the wounds to which many of these women were about to be exposed. She kept it locked in the back of her mind, what could happen to someone exposed to it for the first time — a body, say, disenjoined by shell-fire, or half shorn away, like pulled pork, and where to start with that? No, she had hand-picked these hundred, first hundred of the two thousand five hundred that were to follow, to be administered, and truly ministered, to and by her, from her London office, as they in turn ministered the only care that counts in times such as these: hand-bloody-hands-on wringing wet with sweat-and-death care. The Canadians were here, and they were going to prove themselves better at it than anyone else.

But those padded, palpitating bulkheads! Macdonald frankly giggled at the thought of precisely how her charges' momentary beaus would manage with the big, brass buttons down the front of the dress uniform she had had a hand in designing. This is a side she showed to no one, precisely

because it was so obvious: she liked fun, and plenty of
it, provided it did not interfere with duty. Interfere? It
positively bolstered it! And she had the selfless fondness for
the sisters that only such a motherly position could provide.
She had been young, too; was — still — the life of almost
any shipboard party. Of all the leaders Canada sent overseas
with the First Contingent, Margaret Macdonald was one of
the very few who were "all right" from the start. Knowing
this, she kept it that way.

Jenny was in awe of her: taking part in the Spanish
American War! Or was it the Panama Canal? Then the South
African War … she seemed to run straight at anything that
promised a bloody apron.

"Sister Gray," when Macdonald said it, to Jenny, on parade,
was like being baptized — and lo and behold, the priest was
a woman. A handsome, almost petite, forthright, tactful,
forceful shot right through the axe heads of gender.

Did Jenny go for below-deck gropes — *gropes in groups*,
practically, she said to herself, waddling between sea-sickness
on the one hand and the stench of so much encased flesh
on the other? Well, she told Stan, years later, I was so busy
trying to figure out who-it-was-this-time, the what-we-got-
on-with scarcely mattered. And then, she gave him a big,
sweetheart smile.

"A fine turn-out, Sister," Macdonald went on, recognizing a
kindred spirit in the steady, nervy look behind Jenny's wire-
rimmed spectacles. "If all my sisters were like you, there'd be
scant reason for me."

Laughter, not care, had printed the nascent crow's feet
stepping smartly from her eyes. Nevertheless, she kept a
keen lookout for missing buttons on parade.

44

17

FIRED MEN

STAN COULDN'T quite get it clear in his mind, on the
voyage overseas. Possibly it was because none of the
truly desperate were on the Pilgrimage. Only the socially
acceptables—only those who passed for well. Well, well
enough. He remembered Jenny telling him how, in the
Casualty Clearing Station, during a general action, it got so
she could feel which men were slipping under, which still
cleared the hurdles of death. She read it in more than their
faces—it was as if something moved in on them, clouded over
blankets and semi-shrouded forms, lying in rows on the ground,
like the keys of some great organ, groaning stops of war.

In Toronto it was far more clear. An ex-soldier, say, at
work—from one of the usual resented, resentful cliques of
Returned Men that dotted every company—would start
coming in late, disheveled, absent-minded. His mates, of
course, would cover for him, at first, until it became plain
to them, too: the thing that stalked them all had seized
their former comrade. Everyone carried invisible wounds,
but some began to show before their bodies went into
the ground: shaking, at work; unable to eat, hold their
sandwiches in the lunchroom. An odour about their person.
Fear, the smell of a hunted animal whose hiding place has
been found out. At some point, even the veterans had to
turn their backs, in order to keep their jobs, their self-
respect. In order to keep themselves from going under also.

The fired man would show up in the park across from
work on a workday; Stan might even sit with him, share

confidences none-too-confident. The other would be drinking, of course; drinking or shaking or both — and always, hard up. Small change for what great change was happening — another survivor clawed back, the war reaching out its scabby hand then most when the coast was clear.

If time was stopped for these men, space was frozen solid. There was nowhere to step without pain. One too many patrols into No Man's Land; one too many sharded objects embedded in flesh. And then there was the fact that bullets cannot be faced. They have none. They tear into them — bullets, into faces — but don't introduce themselves. To ask a man, repeatedly, to face the unfaceable was, sooner or later, to unmake him completely.

Worst things last. We all go under, eventually, and just before we cross that line, everyone, and I mean every man jack of us, turns away. The line we cross is in the turning away of others: those we called mate, sister, brother, love. Fine and dandy. But what Stan wanted to know was (You didn't turn on the dimes they begged you for!), what was the incipient cause, and how could you catch it? Maybe, even, make it yours? Was that too much to ask? And of whom? They had faced death, faceless or not, so often it was all out of countenance with them.

The graveyards of Canada were already gorging themselves on government slabs — hillsides of old mates ranged apart from their families, by choice. It scared him more than rising from the fire step: there, at least, in the white heat of fate, you were — momentarily — agent. But this, this obscene slippage, no medal, ribbon, or battalion battle patch could cover it. It meant urinating in doorways and being beaten by police, and even the small Britannic shield on their much-coveted service badges wasn't proof against it.

46

So Stan wore his indifferently, and lost it—frequently. No matter, he passed. Besides, it always came back to him, with its motto, FOR SERVICE AT THE FRONT, running under in sober sans serif; the four dots for the four Corps divisions (he fancied—no one told him that; he was obsessed with meaning); and the initialism, C.E.F., serifed and pointed by the knowledge that no one could wear one of these and not have seen, that. And yet, to the truly broken, even these became badges of shame, and the others hated them for it. Hated and forgave and forgot then, too, how open they had been, how happy to see men other than themselves in the ranks: Indians, Ukrainians, Japanese, Negroes. Not to mention battalions of Chinese labouring in the rear. Jews, Germans (yes), and, sharp as tacks, those we now call Indigenous. All these became progressively *non grata* as the years closed in those who had served—mainstream, sidelined men—who had fought under the Maple Leaf.

His mind was wandering. His stomach was heaving. The thought of lying with Jenny, in a shared cabin of the steamship *Montrose*, nearly made him sick.

18

BURN YOUNG

YOUTH IS LIKE FIRE. While it burns, there is no lack. When gone, lack is all that's left. Now battle, Art reasoned, was the very bonfire of innocence. That bred youth back into their very bones. How was that?

What was *that*? In a second, Stan was beside him, wedged into a forward sap, poring into the chalk dark. A rat? Which one? The oversized animal, fattened on remorselessness, that waddled its way from corpse to corpse, or the hundred-pound cylinder, half-buried in the earth beside them, snuggly sandbagged but safe for no body?

White Star gas. Horror gas. Chlorine and phosgene. Vomit a man to death. They called them rats because they ate everything in their path. Because they were fat. And because the specialists who fauceted their contents into No Man's Land had a habit of abandoning ship after poisoning the waters and stoving every boat on earthen board.

Gas, you see, hangs around. It hugs the earth it kills. And so filled shell craters with toxic gauze you could not wear against anything. Shell craters, Art reasoned, were like rafts in the sea of shoot-me-nots between ... Stan's hand rested, sudden and slow, for a moment on the cylinder, then lifted, like a light barrage, onto the nearest sandbag.

They were that tense, strung from sentry to sentry, sap to sap, and bay to bay, and that finely attuned that they could sense an increase of vigilance in bodies dug into electric attention like fingernails in wet concrete. A certain relaxation in Stan, splayed and spider-eyed beside Art's steady eye-see-youse, lapsed the sergeant back into his proper inquietude. His mind was uneasy, but he let it go, wandering through interstices of terror.

What were they waiting for? A stiff breeze, for one thing, to carry the two contained clouds over. And up. Hill One-Four-fucking-Five. Deal?

Art made everyone younger than they were. He kept his sure, uncertain composure throughout the war: liking what he liked, never insisting. And his—how to say this—equivalence of mind. If it was hard to see how this could be so, Bill reasoned it thus: his company sergeant major simply emptied himself of his own minor contents before battle. Bill, once, looked his friend in the face before they went over, and had the feeling one has returning home, say, to find the family half-buried in the yard, the doors swinging on sepulchral hinges, slamming open shut against the wind and rain.

19

SEX WAS THEM

"I NEVER THOUGHT of having sex *with* them," Lo said, turning the glass in her hand, half full with amber now; her face wry with ex-pat whisky. "I thought sex *was* them. Cutting them away, I mean—the bandages. I thought that was sex, right there."

Lois Archer, former nursing sister turned closet poet, keeper of old flames and still on fire for one of them, gave a sharp look across the bare board table.

"Did I say bandages? I meant their uniforms—what was left of them, that bandaged what was left of them, bereft from them, swept from them and never coming back. Smashed genitalia—you really felt sorry for those, but if there was no face, well, how could you make love to *that*? Afterwards."

Jenny has heard this sort of thing from her friend before—Lois being "outrageous"—her *guillemet* hands thrown up in mock despair. What she listens for are the modulations, changes in what has gone before (the soldiers' torn uniforms as bandages, in this case) and not the obviously provocative (sex *was*).

Listening to Lois was like re-reading a book that quietly resifted its contents overnight, shifting an emphasis here, groping towards a new definition there. There was no malice in this. It fit the rifts in her jagging mind like a tarp over shell-snipped body parts.

She had taken her elocution lessons from the many-mouthed speaking trumpets of her girlhood: the one human voice barrelling broadcast from several flared-epic speaking funnels at once, what was said BOOMing from the stone steps of City Hall, bouncing off Eaton's window griddle, and then, depending on which angle they hit the shop-front sign boards along Queen, each word echoing differently. No matter how swung by the city, or how plain, tawdry, or simply magnificent those signboards were, Lo bestrode their windy variations, Queen of their meanings even as she let them blow.

"But the cutting away?" Jenny asks, her face all attention, sitting across the bare board kitchen table beneath the single bulb, lit and shaded like a luminous croupier.

"Caesarian. *Roma. Amor.* Arms and the man, I don't know. Don't you sometimes feel," Lois says, looking up, her face a little sly, "don't you sometimes feel you could make love to anything, to everything? Those nights when they kept coming, in August, remember? During the Amiens *Offensive*," she said, lordly, and spat out offensive, as if that was all it ever really was, that great victory.

"I'd go out," she continued, aware that Jenny, with her son-of-a-bitch love-match to soldier on with in the dateless, man-free desert of post-war Toronto, might have no further need of her, physically—her physical heresy, "to clear my head from iodine, and there it was, the anodyne of France, those pre-misty morning fields, that indescribable sweetness—or maybe it was the all-smell of congealed blood on me, their blood, the closest anyone can really come to anyone, really ... paint them red with passion—anyway, I'd stand there, and want to slice my own clothes to ribbons, and jump a bush, a cow, a lorry's worth of wounded, anything!"

Jenny was laughing now, her eyes shining. Lois is in her element, which is to say, running stark naked in Jennabeth's head, trailing song words like diaphanous scarves. Isn't this ridiculous? Lo doesn't have to say it, so she does.

"And I'd wish it was you, dear, you with a prick or a prickly pear, I didn't care. Or anybody—it could have been anybody. I swear. Scout's honour," she adds, giving the two-fingered salute, her two fingers crossed for luck, her legs open under the table.

"I know," Jenny says. "Oh, Lo," she sighs, and does not turn away. "I always knew."

They both look at their glasses, and turn.

20

PRODIGALS

Toronto, 1917

CHER PIP:

So. You found another sister. Bigger than me, I bet. And a whole lot more.

I was going to say something. But you took my woman's words away. And I have decided to speak woman and nothing else. This means. See? Anything I want.

I want you, Piperoo, waiting on my every word, not on my only woman. And I hardly was one, when you left. I'm not going to rhyme that.

I've got a new sister, too. I call her Alley-Who. There. Are you happy now you can run off with your very own. I am learning how to go everywhere within my room at once.

Alley certainly does; she loves back places—especially mine. Now don't you worry, even the moon works shifts these days; she's never out when we're in. Prodigals.

Today I saw the city reflected in the sky; it was upside down, chimneys groping towards me, like roots uprooted but still reaching for. I decided it was reaching for you.

Me, too
Love you
Sapanalleyway

21

HARLENE

IT STARTED INNOCENTLY ENOUGH. At the Front, she
would show up when and wherever Bill had managed to go
to sleep. Corporal Ostic hardly slept, but when he did, he
could drop off anywhere. In a war where it was not unheard
of (although who would hear — anything, after this?) for
gunners to sleep beneath their guns *as they fired*, where
soldiers were billeted in heaps, in windy outbuildings, in
airless holes in the ground masquerading as dugouts, or,
sometimes, after forced marches through the night ("Let the
men rest on their packs, Sergeant") they'd tumble onto the
town square, or part down the middle of a sunken road and
ditch themselves till roused (if it was dry enough) …

Helmets off. Was Bill's scalp "dry" as well? That was just
the kind of thing she would come round asking about.

She would find him — though not by his hair, which was
invariably kept so short on the sides you could barely see it.
As for the top — which hardly anyone ever saw for helmet,
cap, or balaclava — it was already thinning on this young, old
man. Bill was 23 when she first came to him, with her ample,
auburn (that's the colour Bill gave it in his mind) tresses,
that oval glow where no woman had blown in before.

No, she would find him, as she once told him, by the quality
of his mind, something she called his "underhair." About
once a week, wherever he happened to have half-curled his
overtired limbs, puttees-be-damned, beneath a sheltering welt
of out-gauged sludge, of she would, simply, appear, dressed (as
far as Bill could make out) in nothing but curls.

Early this particular morning, in the D Sector Polygon Switch between Arfleurs and Sainte-Endivion, she found him sidewise on the fire-step, his rifle between his knees, as if he were prepared, on a moment's notice, to blow his own brains out. The Lewis gun he kept in an oilskin sheath he'd made himself out of captured enemy rain capes.

"Oh, William," she said, letting an Edenic finger pry its way between helmet and scalp, "it is sufficient that you are troubled with any form of hair 'ailment,' or—"

"Wait a minute, Sister, where did you—"

"Or that," she went on, with a light brill of severity, "you desire to improve the appearance of your hair."

"Begging your pardon, Sister, but what in the sweet fuck-up-Satan's-anus are you doing here?"

"Young women can maintain their hair in abundant beauty," she continued, thought, and then changed tack completely, producing a fully wrapped package from behind her—

"ACCEPT THIS WONDERFUL GIFT!" she barked out, then blushed and demurely added, "There is no restriction to this gift distribution."

"Sister, do you have a ... sister? I mean, how come there's always only one of you, and how in fuck's kingdom do you find me every time?"

"I'm not from fuck's kingdom, Corporal. I am the way. The 'Harlene' Way," she serenely explained, and then, as if stuck from behind by a very sharp stick, shouted, "MILLIONS PRACTICE HAIR DRILL!"

"Where's the manual?"

"Every man desires ..." she began, recomposed, then decomposed, then tore open the package with her teeth and spit the paper away, which took Bill more aback than anything else she did or did not do. He had seen soldiers pull pins from Mills bombs with less ferocity. Shaking out her mane of hair (can you believe Bill actually looked away as she did so?), she at last regained her composure.

"Every man desires to preserve a fresh, smart, crisp appearance, and in this respect, the care of the hair is essential," she went on, and then handed him a small booklet (produced, as far as Bill could tell, from the nape of her neck) with four words on the front board: "Hair Drill" in sans serif bold face, and at the bottom, in some kind of baroque, nuptial font: "New Edition." Bill opened it. It was a manual for the tactical employment of Lewis guns. He looked up to tell her, but she beamed right through him — his whole body warmed in the sun of her slumber-wonderful, hirsute cascade.

"No hair trouble can defy the soothing, strengthening effect of 'Harlene,'" she added, winking the two forefingers of each hand around the oft-quoted word. Then she leaned forward, so that he had to see at least the swell of her breasts.

"Do not talk too much about things that cannot be seen," she whispered, urgently, then turned, and as she turned, brushed the cobwebs from his still sleeping ear.

"Fuck," Bill said. He was wide awake.

22

COLLECTIVE GHOST

WHAT IS IT LIKE to lie with a collective ghost? To reach
out your hand and touch, actually touch, what everyone
around you merely wants to be there? Mary Helen wasn't
sure what she had woken with, at first. It was as if she'd
been drugged, or drunk, but no hangover hung over her but
him — he had, John sweet blessed Audet Herald had — in
the night, and now there was this arm — I'm not going to say
impossibly — *impossibly* thrown over her ribcage, elbowing
into her solar plexus with the persistence of gravity.

He smelled like sweet hay. He breathed like a toy
locomotive, a working one that you could ride: she could
scent the oil, felt the boiler of his infant pistons resting
on their haunches, stretched out along the siding of this
bed — flower-strewn; wild-lace — this morning, this day.
She would be late for school. She would never have to
teach again.

"As real as all that?" she had heard herself ask, the day he
slung her in his arms, her wisp of grin sliding into a smile.
Could it be she was actually talking shape-shop with this
existential drifter? She held him at arm's length, her hands
on the forearms that felt her waist, beneath the gingham and
cloth — her breathing, in and out, the porch of their desire.
Those nights before he left, in uniform as he was now, and
no one to stop them from sitting alone.

"I gotta — "

"I know," she said. "You have to stall and feed your horse.
You can take him over to Fred Abercrombie's, he's got a — "

"Old Fred," he said. Old Fred who hadn't passed fifteen when John enlisted. "He married, now?"

"No, John." There. She said it. John. And he seemed almost to relax that much more into being, his hands back on the horse, which turned to show—

"Oh, my stars," she said. A huge, red wound—jagged, something sticking out of it, blood all the way to her fetlocks. Then nothing.

"Is she wounded?"

"It's all right," John said, emotional now for the first time, she could tell by the way he turned his face. "She's not like that all the time. You can see it. No one, hardly anyone else, can."

"What about you." Stated—not a question. John stopped; did he actually fade away? Or was it the strength of the sun, swarming the air with wish dust? "You, John."

"I came back to see you."

"Exactly. I see you. Who else? I've heard rumours."

John smiled again, only this time it looked more like a grimace. He didn't seem to know what to do with the question, as if it threatened his hold on reality.

"There's this horse. My—horse," he added, stupidly. "She's mainly—my horse, but sometimes ..."

"She flies around at night, giving rides for free?"

"Something like that."

"Like what?"

"She's fast."

"How fast?"

"Fast enough."

Oh, those conversations with John! Came trotting back like pale hounds, their monosyllabic paw prints, deft, precise, spelling out how life was going to be before he wasn't anymore. There isn't anymore, anymore.

"You take her over to Fred Abercrombie's," she repeated, and he came back into focus. "He's got a stable. A *stable*. When you're back," she added, a slight sing-song slipping over the harsh husk of her voice—as if willing it to be true, in the magic spells of girls—"there'll be dinner on the table." And, saying this, she turned, half-turned, on the balls of her feet.

"You don't worry about anything, now, Mary Helen," he replied; not darling, not Emaiche. Her full name, relearning how to say it. "I'll take her over and then I'll be back."

"Will you, Johnny?" Facing away now, looking out the window above the sink.

"I've come a long way to reach you."

"I suppose you have."

She was almost relieved to see him go.

23

THROUGHWAY

THE COLONEL had other reasons for leaving his narrow, contiguous, middle-class home in Toronto. It was one of a row of five with a 19th-century carriageway running through the middle, and it epitomized a number of the city's best urban qualities: its slender, compact, decorous refusal either to take up too much space or, conversely, be moved; its surprising spatial savvy in a neighbourhood that could still, in summer, swaddle most of its rooftops with leaves; and—something that has become very hard to find, even here—its easy throughway to the past without compromising—I was going to say—but compromise isn't the word at all: Toronto's past, its arduous order, positively aided its present, just as Allward dreamt his army of the living aided by an army of the dead.

For once, I don't mean Stan. For once, I mean the Allward most Canadians—if they know anything at all about the memorial atop the ridge at Vimy—know best: Walter Allward, the sculptor. To say that Stan was no relation is, strictly speaking, true. But they found kin in that army of the dead—indeed, every member of the Corps, whether they survived the war or not, sooner or later became a part of it. These were not recalcitrant ghosts: they carried arms and swarmed up Vimy with the quick and their own opposites—the Germans, their dead contingent must also have been in play.

To most contemporaries, the visions they had, the real visitations that cannot be gainsaid, when they saw their mates, these latter did not say they were at peace. They said, rather,

Finish the job. Here — we, the dead, we will help you. We'll yank you out of dugouts about to be targeted, tell you when your number's up. No promises, but this: Promise us you will finish it in Berlin, not with Jerry on the run; finish it in ways that will ensure there can never be another one. Beat them down. Send them home pulling horse carts. Those soldier-ghosts did not come back to Canada; they remain in the great unstate of their bones, their bone-yards, the shards of whatever anchored them here long since blown by repeated upheavals.

If anything haunted the Toronto Stan knew, it was that handful of privileged reactionaries who first set up shop in long, narrow lots reaching far (but not too far) into the bush beyond the lake's edge. Simcoe's noblesse much obliged to make you obli-damn-gated. The Family Compact: Cronies from the Macaronis. They were not family. They never would be. They were like the block of narrow houses bricked together on Boulton, in the second of which from the left, the Colonel made his home. He was a widower when Constance grew up into the young mother she now was, and she was as proper as Arthur had raised her to be, a latter-day imperialist with democracy on the side, which is precisely why, when the Colonel made his home home to the men he had come to love, all hell broke loose.

What did this mean? It meant feet that smelled like rotting fruit and clothes that reeked of excrement, men who lived on gin and who could not die too soon, missing persons who subsisted on nothing and pissed on everything, were treated more lavishly, more respectfully — indeed, with more naked love — than Constance had or would ever know from her father or from anyone else. It was worse than having Christ as a roomer; it was like discovering God the Father had been Dad all along, only, not for you.

✹

And so Stan had found him, Colonel Arthur Earnest Leading, D.S.O., A to Z, and, occasionally, S.O.B., sitting S.O.S. on the curb in front of the new Union Station: aged icon washed up on an island of foolscap and valises—bundles of battalion newspapers, 10&th Association magazines—even batches of old orders, scribbled and saved and brought over the waves from a world away.

He took him in, of course. He and Jenny both, to the house on Sullivan Street. Leading expected the back room at the top of the stairs. They gave him the study, on the second floor, its window facing south, overlooking the street—the best room in the house. It was a museum. Stan had transferred Sap's artwork to it. There was plenty of floor for the army cot that Jenny hauled up the stairs. The Colonel stood there, flanked by his new hosts, looking at the walls and the space they made, the former coffered with picture frames, the latter a-fly with pasteboard shapes.

"She wasn't much of a draughtsman, was she?"

"She didn't draw … things, generally," Jenny intervened.

"She drew what happened when she drew," Stan added.

"Did she indeed," Leading said, lost, already, in one picture after another, as if inspecting new troops for the first time. Jenny looked at Stan. Stan shrugged. Battalion sweetheart? Alive or dead, the Colonel got a daughter again the moment Jenny, taking leave of him, touched his shoulder and quietly—as if not to wake anyone—shut the door.

24

SAPPAGE

—No Date—

Herr Stanson von Pipperoon:

You've put an old man into my room. *The* old man, as it
turns out: that old seducer. I think he's worried about the
past. He should be. I think he thinks I'm going to jump from
his head one of these bald moments, just to keep up the
family business. I think he thinks I'm going to tell on him.
Well, I will. He's a dear old dinosaur, Pipsqueek—and he's
your future, if you don't knock it off with your precious past.

Allyoshious? Nope. Alleyambidextera? Nope. Alluminatio
mea? (I hope!) Nope. We keep on guessing what to call
each other. I call you Brother, Officer, Hero. You call me Sap,
because I extend into that No Man's Land you call women
and mistake for the Front. Because I am as forward as you
can (paradoxically go back but actually) go and still be
protected.

Belatedly (get it?),
Sappest

PS: Don't worry overmuch how this one made it to your
mailbox so late in life; the postman is an old soldier—you
know the one, lance-jack I think, who still wears his service
medals in public and his dress uniform to deliver the mail?

PPS: Don't even think of any dead-letter office jokes; I'm
way ahead of you.

25

DAMP GASPER

THE SHIP PITCHED and rolled, and Bill rolled with it, right out the cabin door—like a damp gasper (sea-sodden cigarette) thrown from the pack (magazine)—into the bulkhead (fucking wall of the ship), and, eventually, on deck (sway world under God's raining dick), where he emptied the contents of his Belgian rattlesnake (Lewis gun) or, rather, stomach (*sinktus innardae*) before assuaging the railing with his two-taloned, sluices-open, Lewis-gunner grip.

"A rough night, Mate." It was Art Cane, his former sergeant-on-the-farm, who had, as so often in war, materialized at just the moment Bill was ready to go ape-incapable.

"Heard you bang up the gangway like a loose shot-locker, Mate."

"Sorry, truly, Mate," Bill replied, then rough-heaved more void into the trough of no relief. "*Surgere*," he pronounced, and wiped away a sleeve.

"What's that?" Art was half deaf, and the weather wasn't helping, either.

"Latin for vomit."

"Ancient upchuck."

"Yeah."

"What you got that's worth tossing at this hour, Mate?"

"No relief."

"Never was."

"Not on time, at any—"

"Except that one—"

"Except that time they targeted—"

"The fucking latrines."

"They targeted the—"

"Fritz took them for mortar pits, and our relief—"

"To our very own sweet relief—"

"Came Corporal Constipation and his gut-sized Stokes Mortals."

"The singeing seven?"

"The very. And their outsize, medieval, horse-toss machine."

"The irreverential outhurler."

"Able to puke five miles into Fritz's very fuck farms!"

"Where his bastardization of lay *Belges* … having sated itself on fetal *fricassée à la* Spanish manner … found at last—"

"And on time—"

"The sweet, shite, good-night it unfucking well deserved."

They both said, Amen, so as not to be heard.

26

GRAVE THING

"AH, BUT IT'S A GRAVE THING, to be in love, in the wars."

The old woman strokes Stan's cheek, once. He doesn't know who she is. The Lady Dowager So-and ... so much for that, she's gone. Stan had been waiting for Jenny, in the Jardin de Luxembourg, among the potted trees and broken *Poilus* — or was that the once-potted *Poilus*, the trees now so broken, at the Front, that seeing them whole is almost a novelty. No Man's Land was just a strip, but what a studied strip! Like a poem you read too often, to keep it fresh.

Now, in Stan's lap, his gloved and capped lap, lay the poem he was working on, because Jenny was here, with him, to see it. It was a sestina — a very complicated verse form, he had added, when she'd frowned at the word. And when she went off for a moment, Stan had sat, unknown to himself, framed in this elder lady's eyes: scrap in hand, khaki-dabbed into the fading palette of a Paris never again to be so *gaie* as to pointillize the whole spectrum of the West. Paris, Spring, 1918. Ah, love in public places. Nothing to guess — goodness grace us — about this boy.

"Do you read poetry?" she had asked. He nodded. "And write it, too, I think," she added, both sagely and supercilious at once. And then, "Read it to me," she said, in a voice and tone that would not be denied.

"It begins in the main floor of the building in which we're staying."

She held up her hand. "Read it to me," she repeated, then withdrew her hand, raised her head, and closed her eyes.

CIRCLING THE SQUARE

What we need contains us like the stairs.
Up down, up down, the little girl said,
and the mother, almost as beautiful,
smiled at me when I answered her —
Up down, up down. Most of life is measured
in love, but will only fit in dutiful

rounds of square bashing. Duty will
make a man love you ten times nature,
Wellesley (the Duke of Wellington), fed
on food for powder, famously, said —
and goodness knows, he was actually there,
when sheaves of redcoats, beautiful

in death, gave their lives for beauties dull
as the posts they died at, swathed on hills
just low enough to show that they were there,
serried in runless rows, runed by nature
to decipher duty until they were dead,
and even beyond that call. I was lead,

as they were, to love what cannot be said —
my god, my goodness, but war is beautiful —
until our bodies paint their own coats red,
not to hide, but to make war redoubled:
turnbacked, faced in different colours,
but with the same, ardent, make-ready stare

of men who are already dead. That is where
I came from, knowing what it is to be led
well. And when all is lost—with the Colours
cut down for shame and packed as booty—fill
my heart, assail my terror, love-duty, drill
me in place and let it still be said—

they did not know they loved so died instead—
up down, up down—in sheaves of red. Will
your little feet bare their narrow shoulders,
thrust up under monuments stone dead,
with eyeballs like black and white marbles?
One could do worse, for love. For valour

casts cannon into crosses, newly minted,
makes up love from losses, and who can kill
that? Make war, my love; lie down, my beautiful.

   A pause. Jenny stood just behind Stan, who had, for the
moment, forgotten she existed.
   "Young man," the woman began sternly, then softened.
"Sex isn't as bad as all that." The latter she directed at Jenny.
They all looked at each other.
   "Ah, but it's a grave thing, to be in love, in the wars," she
said again, touched his cheek, and then, wheeled away like
antique stars.

27

UTTER NIGHT

SAP HAD BROUGHT the torchlight, but Alley brought the rope, the rope she tied around the wire handle of the storm lantern, to lower it, level with her friend, as she clung and wrung herself down the horseshoe ladders to the little splash her boot-heels made as they hit-slipped on the not-quite-frozen bottom of the creek. To shine your light on smallness itself; to find that you have less, much less, room than you thought — Sap had never experienced anything like it. Light the lamp of midnight, expands the room; lantern down the rabbit hole, not one bit better than your worst nightmare, and no bunny in sight. Or if there were, encased in racing its way through brickwork warrens, very, very late. She reads seams of pointing with her fingers, no text there, but the texture of the faint yellow brick, that comforts her.

But the going down, the going down, was like sinking, really sinking, in the earth as element. The rungs, the narrowness, and the jolt of blue terror that kept Sap a brick herself in order to get through it, all contribute to it. She wobbles a little, does not fall. She looks back up through the pillar of night above her and, holding the lantern in one hand, grabs the torch in her pocket, turns it on with her teeth, and shines it up the way she came.

To Alley, looking down, it's as if a glow-worm burrow-burns up at her; as if there were comfort in the grave; as if desire, which had hitherto seemed only up, suddenly dove into a whorl of cold, and winked. Come die, come die. And it's only as she touches bottom that she feels fully how

deeply mad this idea of theirs actually is. Sap had hatched
it at the kitchen table, red-eyed at the kitchen table, after
the horse officers had gone, taking with them the one thing
she thought to steal from war—her pet pig. Flavella, named
after the Head of the Imperial Munitions Board, Sir Joseph
Flavelle; Flavella, the slaughterhouse survivor; Flavella, the
Hogtown escapee.

Early one evening, the spring just past, Sap took the long
way home to Sullivan—home from volunteering at Liberty
Munitions, musing on spherical balladry, her lyric trajectory
flung overseas.

SHELL SONNET

These belts that belt their belting up so high
  from wheels above return to wheels below,
  whose lathes and shavings, vessels stacked in rows,
prognosticate the falling of the sky.

We hold within this hallowed, hollow hall,
  a honeycomb of turned and tapered bells
  lacking clappers—a sea of soundless shells
stacked and serried, we cannot hold them all—

that spill onto the sidewalks of the streets:
  banks whose rivers we their workers are,
  and they our awful infants, lifted clear

across the ocean, swaddled under sheets
  of snow that powder their procession white.
  But black will fill their mouths and utter night.

28

NO MISTER

"Mister Herald," Leading went on, as he had been taught, to address anyone under the rank of captain, Mister, "you were expressly seconded to the one-oh-eighth to lead our scouts and raiding parties into No Man's Land."

"Yessir," John replied evenly, looking his new colonel right in the face—as opposed to straight in the eye, which would have struck the former as too intimate and the latter as insubordinate.

"Your reports are a little vague, at times" (Leading had no idea that Herald was practically illiterate, that his reports were, in fact, dictated to one Lieutenant Stan Allward, who deliberately typed them badly, scrambling the grammar and messing with the consequence of letter and letter, word and sentence and word, lest John should be caught out and forced to write on his own) "but your findings, as confirmed by either you or members of your party, in person, have put us neatly down Fritz's front end. Your former colonel speaks so highly of you I was almost loathe to take you from him, but it's no secret we've had some trouble beyond the wire," Leading added, with genuine shame. "Now, this gas affair is the biggest, bravest, boldest thing to happen since Mars fucked Vesuvius—"

It was Venus, sir. John didn't say it. But the slightest shift of manner, which Leading caught, was enough to reign him in.

"Everyone in the 4th Division is in it ... or parts of all of it is—I won't hide from you ... there have been some ... reservations." He was thinking, specifically, of colonels

Kemball and Beckett, of the 54th and 75th battalions, respectively. The former found the wind unpredictable; the latter felt the raid was no secret. Arthur paused, looked down for an instant, and said, almost to the map spread in front of him, on the little dugout table in the second line of Allied trenches before the wan mass of Vimy Ridge, "What are yours?"

"We've been assured that the gas will only be used in the event of a strong wind," Herald replied. There was a long, awkward pause.

"And no one can assure that," Leading conceded. Major Stock, his adjutant, made small gestures of impatience.

"Given that the gas has to be pushed uphill," Herald replied, with a flash of appreciation, "and that there are to be two clouds, the one following the other, after a pause ... of forty ... fort-*tee*—minutes, sir."

"The gas cylinders are *in*, Mister Herald." That wasn't Leading. It was Stock.

"Yessir, they are most certainly *in*. The front line trench. And they have the wind up on every man on post, for fear a shell may do more than stray from overhead. Do you know what it's like to stand posted for four hours beside a tank of acid air? An obvious one, at that? Trying to disguise them with sandbags just makes them more whumpy. The Germans can see them, sir; they have the high ground; they listen to our working parties as well as we do theirs. They know, sir," Herald finished, switching his sirs from Stock back to the Colonel, who mused, sat down, put a hand to the back of his head.

"Thank you, *Lieutenant*. Now, Misterrr ... Allward—"
"Sir."

"What's your opinion. Does Fritz know we're going over the bags with gas our argument?" Leading always becomes more literate when he speaks to me, Stan thought. And he thought, too, of the first cases of gassed men he had ever seen, so saw instead the tarnish it left on their brass buttons. He stopped thinking.

"I fear gas more than Jerry himself," Stan said, as surprised as anyone present at his frankness. "And I trust Lieutenant Herald's judgment better than my own," he added, needlessly. In matters such as these. But that would have been even more needless to say, and, needless to say, they went over, anyway.

29

FIRST RECOIL

BEING HIT IN THE HOLE that was supposed to hide you,
to be buried alive by the very fire that drove you under in
the first place, and then to be dug out, literally, from your
dugout, well, that, for many, was quite simply the last straw
in a world of fears and humiliations, not to mention real
deaths and mutilations, that had already chased all sense of
depth from most men's minds.

Say that one could even say it, as I just have; say that one's
reader was every bit as sympathetic as you are, still you
would lack — thank Christ and all his saintly subterfuges — I
say you would lack, still, that primal deracination, pistoned
kickback which reduced the world to an ever-shifting series
of two-dimensional objects laid awry and shaken askew,
shuffled by blasts or bombardments, but nowhere to hide
or take shelter. Everywhere opaque and translucent at once,
exposed to that terrible light, the sunburst of whizz-bangs in
the doorway, the end of everything that once held the power
to hide.

Stan stood a long while beside the captured German gun,
looking at it, laying his hands on it, feeling its weight in
the beads of mist congealing on its iron sides. These "long,
talkative animals!" Fists of silence. Ha. To think that such
monsters once moved! To think — we all — moved, made
choices, dug each other out of depths ineffable. In-effing-
capable, un-effing-able. At first, we did it because we were
actually alive and wanted to go on living — wanted others to
have the same chances (chance, it must be said, had become

something that Stan absolutely hated). Then, it became more or less second nature, the result of training, practice, repetition and (not least) reputation. But after these reasons had cleared for naked terror, settling down like a sucker on the brain, there was still the blind inclination to go on fighting for a world forever lost in the hope that somehow it would re-exist, or pre-exist, for other people, some day.

The men and women of 1914–1918, had in themselves that saturation in precept (followed by real sensibility) that took—and held—long after their actual, individual capacities to feel were blasted to oblivion. It wasn't complicated. It was like the progressive deafness from that came from firing one of these.

How strange that he should have outlasted this ungainly earth shaker! By the shock of that first recoil, as the monster shot back on pistoned haunches—so plainly fucking the firmament—one could empty all the wombs in the world.

30

SEX IN HEAVEN

"How many, do you think, are going to show up?" Lois asked.

"Sex in heaven," Jenny answered.

"Is not all it's cracked up to be," Lo retorted.

"Maybe eight, depending on whether or not they got laid up."

"Don't get carried away, missy."

There was a rap on the door, followed by the closeted uproar of intimates who see each other once in the bluest moon—a kind of subdued, preverbal howl, like two alley cats devouring charity—followed by Lois's liquid, easy prologue:

"Grace Maria. *Gram.*"

The way she received visitors at these gatherings made each arrival feel like the hoped-for, unexpected extra. These were women she knew well (knew by nickname, if such applied) but greeted them first with their given names, in full, followed by how they were known to the world—nothing theatrical or exaggerated, eschewing the patronymic, but never patronizing.

"Sophia Anne. *Sophie.*"

Shapes emerged from behind bundled bodies; galoshes shared a growing still life on the main mat in the hall; damp berets clustered together like toddler jellyfish.

"Clare Louise. *Clare.*"

One by one, they sounded out, within the largely empty house on Jarvis Street where Lois had grown up. Their hard, sensible shoes beat the silence from the hallway and then consigned it to the root cellar with a progressively louder recognition scene in the kitchen, as each sister swept in and took a chair around the table.

"Florence Rachel. *Flossie.*"

The single bulb, with its wide green shade hovered above them, its light descending from the ceiling like a *Deus ex machina manqué*—as Lo would say—neither strong enough to be harsh nor pale enough to forgive. Above it, the walls glowed a faint green. Under water, Lois thought; at sea, Jenny silently rejoined, but swept their *Llandovery Castle* metaphors out of mind with the first knock.

"Elaine Agnes. *Aggie.*"

The tumblers from which they drank were all sorts and sizes—chintzy souvenirs from Lois's travels after the war—Niagara Falls being a common theme, with naughty-but-nice girls draped over the wreck of the old scow or swinging from riparian railings—*Come and Take Me for a Ride! ... How Now, Ground Scow?... No Scowling!*—but the hooch they poured into them had the swift, stern effect of blurring the differences, not to mention the danger of their various appeals.

"Millicent Marjory. *Pearl.*"

Lo was an only daughter who inherited everything when her solicitor father died—of heartbreak, really, heartbreak—after cancer took her mother. That had determined her: it was either nursing or nothing. Not even the books that lined the father's empty study—Wordsworth and Shelley, Ruskin and Rossetti—could hold her back. She had trained at Victoria Hospital in Montreal, and was on board the *Franconia* with the First Contingent by the fall of 1914.

"Alice Amelia. *Ammy.*"

Lo was not a natural — or so she thought — until the fascination took hold, the doing of it, while a living, breathing, broken body lay open under ether and her own ministrations counted like fate. And, when she returned, she, like almost all of her colleagues, could no more imagine becoming a wife than she could sew her own head on backwards.

Besides, all the best men are dead.

"Dead, or deeded," Gramm adds, who has come from Love Avenue in Toronto's east end. "I live on love," she likes to say. "So, why can't I get any?"

Some, like Jenny, were social workers, bound to the same wheel that whirled the soldiers into Returned Men; some nursed in private homes; some even walked the corridors of the Christie Street Hospital, where the ones who could not … what? *Recover*? They made it home. What then? Couldn't reach the street. Could be in Toronto for the rest of their mortal lives, unable to so much as block the sidewalks with the ghosts of their shot-off limbs.

These men, these men! Carried a Toronto within them that aged by hints through the too-bright-by-half brick-fenestration-be-damned windows, like a recent widower whose hair, for the longest time, goes only slightly white. As the city grew louder, the hospital walls waxed thinner. As the men grew older, their mates waned. But each night, beyond the clarity of one thousand bells, one thousand Krupp guns erupted over them, and they waked like premature chicks to wade through the yoke and shell of their undoing.

And the sisters, sworn to silence, the pale blue of their service uniforms a tightly knit sky where no birds sang, were as dutiful daughters whose message was the dark of their —

"Oh no, that will not do at all!" Jenny breaks in, impatient of my poetry.

How about, hushed as nuns, they carried their last cries in their bosoms like splinters of the true —

"Christ, yes, but no good," says Lo, at ease with the content, but not the manner. She takes a long, deep drag, then stubs her cigarette into a ceramic frog. "Thrills," to start with, she says, and settles her eyes on me. "It was *thrilling*."

"And the closer to danger, the better," Jenny adds.

"Nothing you'd want to see — even once," Lo continues, lighting another. "What's to talk about?" She throws the match to the floor, still burning.

"Do you know what it's like to be on the receiving end of a battle in a C.C.S.? There's no ... military moment to it, as in, *The moment they rose from the trenches will always remain sacred in the memory of those few who survived it.* There are no sacred moments for you to drape your forlorn form against and say, Ah yes, that was the time Charlie tore his dressing from his thigh! *Head Wounds As I Saw Them; Abdominals I Have Known; Ripping Ravages.* It's a *hospital,* you're trying to put things back to the way they *were.* There's no possible forward narrative that doesn't search, desperately, back at the same time, like the memories of each individual of how a human body ought to feel."

"Also, we were really on our own. Battle, for us, was not a communal event," Jenny adds evenly. "So, on the one hand, you have whatever goes on in there — indescribable, really, not to mention unfair to whoever's broken self was trying to organize itself in the midst of ... things missing. And after, there's teas, outings, hut mates, and "home" sisters taking care that our collars and cuffs are white for our half-day off each week."

Or cavorting like a pair of half-frocked Amazons, I want to say, but don't.

"I bet you didn't think we'd break in like that," Lo says, smart-alecky, letting a cool jet of smoke stab the space in front of her like a searchlight.

"Who is Matron here?" Jenny asks, turning back to her sisters in time. They all raise their glasses at once.

31

ONE OVER EASY

THE TROUBLE BEGAN, not surprisingly, with the horse. Or, not the horse, for who knows what John Herald led to Fred Abercrombie's stables that drifting day in the high summer of 1936? Say, rather, that the trouble began with the horses, Fred's, or that they sensed the trouble first, as animals generally do.

Now, Fred's sister came in from Winnipeg with her 6-year-old daughter in tow, Fred's wisecracking sister widowed on the whim of a wet night by a whiff of pneumonia strong enough to snatch her well-to-do husband away, away when they were visiting friends—in *Gananoque*, of all places, her mother used to say in that flapper-banter way she had, as if one chose where one died—and Hope Jolie was left fatherless and Margaret had to shift from boarding house to boarding house and whack and thump her way back into the workforce while she whacked and thumped her single charge into good grades, solid posture, and attention at the piano.

H.J. had been a noisy baby, but became a very quiet child, besieged by angora sweaters no one knew she was allergic to and tripped up by her mother's high living crossed with her even higher expectations, high-balled by the hooch she always hid when Fred pulled up outside in his ... but today, there was no car come to fetch them from the train station in Carman. Fred pulled up in his buckboard, patent reminder to the great, panting engine that its power was still measured by horses.

Margaret, for once, let Hope run, and she ran to Fred like the father he'd never be. And he held the stubby persistence of his favourite niece up for all to see like a prize sheaf of wheat.

"Look at this! Or am I Miss-Stook!" It was him all right, the big man who didn't die, the only one to make her feel small in the way that big little girls love — light enough to be uplifted, up, up, high on the wagon and higher still, seated in her uncle's lap, following the tarped rumps of Basker and Double-Bride, Fred's best working team.

The trouble had begun when Fred went to get the horses. It wasn't just that they had been nervous in their stalls, they took fright on the road at almost nothing — in the way that horses will but more so, for no unreason at all: no unexpected shadows, no objects unforeseen. Heading home to Roland, Hope Jolie had eventually to sit on the feed sacks with her mother while Fred called and cajoled, *Ho Basker, Hey-hey Double-double,* and heat hit the Prairies like the flat iron of Juno herself.

They took fright at being led back in, too, and it was then that Fred saw there was hay in a crib where no horse was kept. Now, come evening, with the Pritchards over for supper and a glad if somewhat dry Margaret presiding over a game of One Over Easy, Fred heard what sounded like gunfire. It was Double-Bride kicking her stall and Fred knew that, but by the time his deliberate stride took him to the stable gate the four living horses within had just about gone berserk.

It was as if a windstorm had turned electric within the very barn. They didn't just see Blaze for what she was, they saw and smelt the blood, and then Fred saw, in the stall where John had tethered her, saw, and turned away; turned, and saw again, and then wrestle-led his four animals out into the yard and let them tear up the dirt while he went looking for a mop and pail. Something had bled into the hay where Blaze had lain.

It was then, as Fred crossed the yard from the barn, that he saw Mary Helen standing uncharacteristically on his porch with a rhubarb and peach pie wedged into the either side of her. She never came over after dusk and certainly not on a Saturday evening but there she was, with an odd satisfaction in the cant of her whole demeanor and Fred just sensed it as the horses had sensed and felt Blaze coming amongst them with her quarry of fate.

And she, Mary Helen, without so much as a hiccup from one heartbeat to the next said, "Oh, Johnny was by I meant to ask you, is it all right if he stables his horse with yours?"

And Fred, without so much as a Johnny-what-horse looked her full in the face. "The dead don't rise until it's time, Mary; they don't rise until He returns." And when she frowned into the silence following, "Do you know who's been mucking around in my stables?"

It had been John's job to do it before the war but nothing under any sun or moon was going to give that current credence in Fred's steady mind. The porch door creaked its bone-xylophonic shring.

"Mary Helen, this is Hope Jolie, Margaret's girl."

H.J. gravely held out her hand; Mary Helen as gravely took it and slowly shook it.

"What grade are you in, Honey?"

"Four."

"What's your favourite subject?"

"Mommy says I do best in French and Latin."

"But which do you like the best?"

"Fingerpainting."

Fred laughed, put a hand on H.J.'s over-whumped shoulder. "That was always my forte," he added, and even Mary Helen snapped-to for the instant. Fred never said forte.

"You tell John," he says, shifting his ground for hers, "You tell John he can't keep her here. He can pasture her in the far quarter, in the old shed."

Fred doesn't say this because he believes John is returned; he believes some shenanigans are underway that he must play along with for now, plod along beside her plot of wrong, young, gone loss — and hope she doesn't go crazy with grief again. Crazy with grief. Crazy with rage — rage at her for all the grief she would not shed. Stable his horse with mine! Most unstable girl he'd ever met. Maybe that was it. It wasn't. The problem was the doomless cope of his belief that only One Man could come again. Christ did satisfaction on the cross, yes, but only if you read the whole story. Lots of people came back, either doubled or disguised or just plain them.

John stabled Blaze where she belonged, after that. And so the horses were becalmed — Basker with his black-olive sheen, Double-Bride with those two patches of white haggard on each side — while, every night, high above the far quarter, thunderheads gathered and flashed as something like prairie fire raced across the fencings of the sky.

32

GO BY FEEL

"You actually prefer to go by feel, don't you?"

John says nothing. Looks at the dugout wall. Map of earth, crumbling upright. The shudder-drone of shelling lifts for a moment and they drift, the two of them, on their little patch of under-surface night.

It was starry when they first went out, starry and not a moon shining. And how could he not be mad to go? Every jaking time Herald scouted beyond the wire — before and after the battle for Vimy, around and about Hill 70, or before the Amiens push (there was no after, after that) — Stan contrived to be attached to his party, or just his person.

If I had an infinity of clusters of stars making my pages white from darkness, I would contrive to tell you the fast and loose way John wore his webbing, the pattern his sweat made on his back through the khaki, his disregard, at night, for helmets and even (sometimes) box respirators — if they were in a sector where gas was not already everywhere you sliced your way towards Fritz. I would tell you that Stan's rapture over his friend was due to those things, or to John's complete attention to his surroundings, not a three-sixty circled but a three-sixty sphered, aware not only of what was in fact all around them (munitions and men munitioned to meet them) but which could also upheave from the ground (mines and countermines, of which Vimy had, literally, hundreds) or drop in from above (*Hello, Shellissimus!*).

Most any junior officers, keen for action, wore out after six months; John freshened from exposure: Stan smelled it on him like damp cordite. But why prevaricate with a multitude of specifics? How his deft hands splayed their warning fingers before dangers — sensed, unseen — in the muck; how many times he turned Stan from those minute displacements (head up two hairs too high; foot a toe too far over) that spelled death or at least detection in the dark? Stan was crazy in love, and with a man it hardly mattered; with Jenny somewhere back of the lines even less. This was Athelstan's stone time; this is when he made a bonfire for his machicolations, and poured such seething pitch from his own senses they would sear around John's slightest gesture.

If John knew it (and he did), he made no sign. And Stan never knew how his eyelids' flutter made the flickering moving picture film that John played in his mind, whenever he needed an image of himself to himself.

He did go by feel — a feel that felt out from training itself and which all good soldiers have to some degree — John to an extreme that suggested a raft of seconds: second sight, second nature, an extra life, and which eventually led to his being seconded to almost every trip that men from the 108th Battalion made into No Man's Land. Except, oddly enough, the really big one.

33

CLOUD LAND

STRANGER, if you were to spy on an allied trench in 1917, when there was nothing doing but day and no one to be seen but dun lumps under cover from heaven's eye, would you be surprised to see live men passing time among the clouds?

"Definitely not a donkey," Art said. "More like a dragon."

"Or like a dragoon," ventured MacKay—new to this narrative, and not to be seen or heard from again. This is a common feature of battalion histories: actors appear and disappear, their incorporate lives reduced to a walk-on, because there were simply too many of them, and too many fatalities, near-misses, or just plain missing to keep track of.

"Where do you get that?" ventured a third, whose name will not even be known.

"The way the ears lie back," MacKay again, "and the tail bristles."

"How long have you been on post?" Allward asked, "to see ears on something like that?"

A long pause.

"I dunno," John Herald said, at length. "The necks are right, and the first head is right on target, but the second one is more like an ad for hair drill."

"Fuck off," Bill said.

"That's fuck off, Captain Herald, sir," John corrected sagely. His promotion after Vimy had just come through.

"Fuck off, Captain Sir Fucking Herald ... off, sir," Bill corrected.

Stan, for his part, was trying not to impose, but allow the clouds to reveal. Shapes. Something that is almost impossible to do, especially among those trained to look for specifics in No Man's Land.

And then, Bill was falling skyward. He didn't scream at first, or even call Art, who saw his body suddenly jerk and stiffen of itself, almost as if a bullet had somehow penetrated the earth and hit him through the trench wall. The clouds went racing towards him, as he lay there, frozen with velocity, his eyes wide as the pie-shaped ammunition pans he was used to slapping over the firing mechanism of his Lewis gun. The method of instruction was to strip the gun before you talked too much about it; Bill was indeed stripped — of gravity it seemed and sense to his Mate — but it was Art who did the talking:

"Where are you, Mate? Bill, where in fuck's kingdom are you?"

"Harleeeeeeeene!" Bill wailed.

"Jesus sweet MacMurphy humping Jackson, Jake, and John!" I don't even know who said that one.

Then another — Laverton, for certain ... I think ... "Shut him up, or I will. Fritz will have us hammered in an instant!"

"You take your fucking orders from Fritz!" That was Art. Again: "Corporal Ostic!"

"AAAAAAAAAAAACCEPT!" Bill shouted, open-mouthed as if to howl the clouds open to accept him, coming right up.

"Corporal William Reginald Ostic! The parts of the Lewis gun may be divided into two groups: what are they?" Bill, convulsing now, swallowed, swallowing; Laverton come round the fire bay but without his Lee Enfield.

"WHAT ARE THEY?" he asks. Lynde, who fed him pans of ammunition at Vimy, brings the gun itself to his fever-flailing hands; one he places on the stock, the other, on the radiator for the barrel, air cooled. Lynde says nothing, but the hands stop shaking, begin to feel.

"What are they?" Laverton, gently now. "Come on, Bill, you taught me this stuff years ago." He is, in fact, worried that the Germans will use his comrade's cries as a challenge, a target to hone in on during a lustless day of quiet trust between the lines, but he pays no more attention to the first *tophlattothratt-tophlattothratt* of a Minnie coming over than he would to a summer cicada brought down beside him, kicking on its broad back, overpowered by the same sun that kills us all.

Tophlattothratt-tophlattothratt tophlattothratt-tophlattothratt tophlattothratt-tophlattothratt BANG-Booooooooooooombe!

The first trench mortar bomb, cascading head over heels like a badly thrown football, comes down twelve paces from the front glacis. Dust and dirt scatter over the small party (How many? How can I tell through the acrid-and-overactive fog of war? Herald, Allward, Cane, Ostic, MacKay, Laverton, Lynde, a few others I can't make out—one with the longest hair I've ever seen.) Then, Private Hebib shows up, with the actual manual in his quicklife hand.

Tophlattothratt-tophlattothratt tophlattothratt-tophlattothratt tophlattothratt-tophlattothratt tophlattothratt-topthlero BANG-Wh-ANG-BOOOoombe!

The second smashes into a small bivvy just beneath the parados. Debris fussed into the trench as the earth farted scrap into the fire-bay, but there was no one inside—its sleepers had been roused out by Bill's howling. Hebib got down on his knees, on the bottom of the trench, next to Bill, who cradled his weapon lengthwise, a stay, a snapped mast clasped at sea.

"Method of Instruction," he began, correctly omitting the preliminary *the*, "in the *Lewis gun*," he added, for emphasis, as if point size in a document really dictated the volume of one's voice, not to mention the volume of—

Tophlattothratt-tophlattothratt tophlattothratt …

The volume of fire, was what I meant to say. Fritz was getting his distance.

Unfazed, Hebib continued: "Section One. General Description. Name: Lewis Gun. Point three-o-three inches; gas operated and air cooled."

SHHH-WHang! ClAnG!

Bill stopped screaming. His eyes came back into something like focus.

"The gun is divided into two portions," Hebib went on evenly.

Tophlattothratt-tophlattothratt tophlattothratt …

Again. "The gun is divided into two portions, Bill. What are they?"

Tophlattothratt-tophlattothratt tophlattothratt …

"Stationary and moving!" he cried at last. He was an old hand at trajectory; he could tell the next shell was—*Get the fuck out of this bay*—right on target.

And the Minnie fell directly among them.

34

RE-ESTABLISHED

Colonel Leading looked out onto Sullivan Street. It sagged towards Spadina, where, of a sudden, it exploded into serried banks of light. His time spent volunteering at the Department of Soldiers' Civil Re-establishment was over—those interminable days, spent waiting for the next near-hopeless case to stumble through the doors of the Keen Building, coast unsteady palms along the mounting balustrade, and appear in the doorway of those glassed-in offices, frosted against what was only too easy to see: this man had exchanged everything for nothing, had known such joy of intensity as opens on those days of survival in war, to be followed by the stupefaction of city streets, dogs dreaming in the sun on sidewalks, lives carrying on anyway. He had believed, in those first, stumbling-towards moments, that something like hope could be reborn in these men, who had never been established in the first place. *Établi*—it meant a work table, and table, a tablet—the tables of the law. He'd looked that up. Anything to make meaning out of what he was doing, or undoing, or hoping to undo—the workings of the war, which left such unworkables in its tabled wake. For tablets were all that was left of them—lists of the dead, lists of those who had served, in the back of battalion histories: wounds, citations, current fixed addresses, care of Mrs. So-and-So, of Messers Bang and Brittle, last seen in the company of Jupiter and Mars. So much to be recorded! Former occupation, lists of ineligibles, please fill out this, leave us with that, we'll see what we can do.

But there was nothing to be done. All that mattered was to meet their eye, stand up when they came in, shake their hand, offer them a chair. Wear the D.S.O., wear your service badge, and in Leading's case, in the early days, until he saw it was no help—was, in fact, often a positive nuisance to these men's peace of mind—wear the whole shebang: boots, cap, and Sam Browne, as if to say, *I accept you, whatever else may follow*. We have both seen *that*. We have known the moon of night marches, work parties, endless fatigues of front-line maintenance. *Main-tenir*. To extend that certain hand, that had known such authority; to lean attentively into the space no occupation could fill, and act as if not only will but even grace still persisted, in this Lethe of lost nations, whole nations of foreign ecstasy, washed away.

Eventually, even those paid to push these scraps of men into round holes and filing cabinets grew weary of the Colonel's constancy, for they all knew they could offer nothing, and somehow, having someone in their midst offering nothing, for nothing—a volunteer adjustment service where no justment could possibly be made—served to underline their impotence. They could not cross him—he had too many friends among old hands lingering in the doorways that dogged them home. They hid behind the increasing cold of those frosted glass dividers, until one day, Arthur Ernest Leading got up, and decided it was time to up and write it down.

Stan and Jenny made him welcome. It was really the lost hope of him, and her miraculous care, that kept him going, now. Someone to dress for, for breakfast; a house to keep, quietly. Above all a woman's form to wonder at, in the way of old men, grateful not to have been left genderless, men among men, nothing. That she was unhappy, that he had lost his fire, after the Corps Reunion, and their union, grown stale on memories neither could maintain, he knew. That he provided the necessary distraction — How is the Colonel doing today — and that he asked them in turn, made a difference. They shored up their memories, shared a rare drink on Friday evenings, allowed reminiscences to fill the vacancy of one more day away. But now they were gone, gone overseas for the opening of that monument to monstrosity, and left him with the neighbour cat, the morning bread and milk wagons, rag-pickers, and Russian Jews sloping towards Spadina, which churned in gambles of industry and shook like block-long dice.

35

KEEP THAT WALK

ALLEY WAS TO KEEP that walk for good in her heart of
art. She wrapped the two of them, ever upright in the
dank under-tunnels of Toronto, tight around her adult
imagination, like a body-wide, bloody tourniquet—or
an extra belt of iron on a dreadnought. Sap's torchlight
searching out ahead, the pinhole of her vision counterswung
by the storm lantern in Alley's left hand, her right afraid to
feel along the frozen wall, but having to or else.

Beneath them gurled and slooshed neither water nor
ice, but some unguessable refusaliva, entrailing from the
brickwork. They could make out very little, but what they
did see was so well intentioned—the keystoned feeder
mouths elegant and true—as if to say, *We made this for you,
Little Tricklings.*

Brick bonds barrelled around them—the arteries of
Sapphira's father, Fred Allward, who laid in the day-lit city
course after course of red and yellow loaves, like an urban
baker: building maker. Sap told herself that there was air on
the other side, that she and Alley were in a long, long, long
room, Antaean corridor snailing its shelter-heavy way across
the soil. She did this so as not to think how far down they
really were, how far gone from the waning world way up
there. Air, air. Father, farther; father, farther on.

She would never tell him—her hod-held, plumb-tuck,
brick-layered father—that she had been down here, in the
snaky belly of his sure and pointed art, journeying through
its darkest dark.

For Alley's part, she sang snatches of made-up verse:

Sap and Alley underground,
seeping soft, without a sound;
what strong arms will set them free,
lift them out, eternally?

and remembered John Odd, Junior telling her, if it rained, the runoff would come running, crash and splash, a wall of rush, to flush them out beneath the icy bay like spiders in a fire hose. What an image. He wasn't so crazy as all that, she thought and found herself thinking, too, of her first day at the new school her parents had found for her that fall — Sap spying her from the plank fence edging the playground. What was that she called her, long after? *The Runt of the Literal-Minded.*

The actual taunts were rich enough: *Parlour maiden, Alley can,* and — where did this one come from? — *Fish head.* The callous circle of spectators, being pushed backwards over another girl knee-stooled for the purpose and, after a few dud hits, the sudden wailing mane of hair above her as Sap tore the accusers from her chest.

"You'd think they'd pick on someone their own size," Sap said (or something like that — who remembers what, exactly, is said, there and then, after a battle?), and then, looking Alley up and down, added, "only, I don't think any are as small as you."

She hauled her up, then, and almost carried her past the bleeding noses and black-eyes-in-waiting that stood off from them like bested wolves. Girls' love.

36

IT'S ALL RIGHT

Toronto, 1919

Sap —

You. Are not. Here. "It's all right, Athelstan — Mother there, on the walk, the porch strung with bunting and streaming crepe.

"It's all right, Athelstan. Your sister is dead." And then Father. And then it was as if the entire street emptied its contents, hollowed itself over, became a tunnel with wind and dust blowing through. There is no more you. Keeping time in my mind, gravely *pour les heurs*, the ones I no longer have to save for future theres, that are toujours nowhere, now.

Some say pneumonia took you. Some say Spanish flu. I can't believe I'm rhyming this. You're gone. You're gone. Untrue.

SAP SONG (2)

You turned blue; I thought I knew
  the colour, but the why
it should be the death of you
  I'll never know. The sky

turns its blue above me
  to remind me every day:
your agony, your ecstasy,
  before you flew away.

—Stan

37

LIAR

SAPPHIRA MAKES SHAPES from paper; she makes paper cutouts for the tree, because this Christmas, the first Christmas of the not yet Great War, there are no new ornaments for sale: they all came from Germany, along with most of the toys Torontonian children were used to opening on Christmas Eve.

You'd expect, what, cherubs and snowflakes, cribs and natal stars, but the shapes Sapphira makes are unintelligible to Stan, who sits opposite her, a copy of *With the First Canadian Contingent* spread before him on the white kitchen table. They have several heads and multiple eyes, or maybe three wings and a single leg, or monopeds on all four sides, like Plato's happy humans, before sex split them down the middle. Stan isn't even sure of that: Are the heads, wings; do the feet, march? Are there girls and boys in her world? Is Sap, herself, a girl? She calls some Flywheel Angels, others Rolling Soldiers. She turns and turns the folded paper as she cuts, and as she cuts, neither talks nor sings, all intent on the shapes that foliate from her hands.

It can't be *With the First Canadian Contingent*; that book, made to look like a photo album, with letters and poems from the Front (2nd Ypres in particular) and sold to raise money for field comforts, didn't appear until the year following. But Stan is used to mixing things up, as he watches the shapes—mobiles, they'd call them now; mobiles: what would she think of that?—pirouette above him, strung from the ceiling above his bed in St. Julien.

What are they doing here? Jenny must have brought and put them up, overnight, when he was out—baubles above a baby's crib. Still, they work; Stan lies quietly, watching them shift their shadows against the whitewashed walls.

It isn't often Stan does an "Art Cane": scrabbling for his service revolver in the dead of night, the children—of course, there are no children for Jenny to worry Stan might shoot, thank God—wailing from behind their mother's nightdress. Besides, Art doesn't shoot inside the house. He goes out. Mild-mannered Company Sergeant Major Arthur Cane, the most reliable man in the 108th Battalion, stalks past the Church of St. George the Martyr, in downtown Toronto, looking for Germans to kill. The Canes are on the Vimy pilgrimage. They even brought Lucy, their youngest: child of light to the dark old world over the sea.

Sapphira's mobiles sweep their droopy wings, shrug their baseless shapes, querying Stan with their changes. What am I now? A seraph, O Sapphira. And now? A star shell, hovering down. And now? A coal box bursting above us on the march—and then they all sway the same way aflutter, as Jenny pushes the door open and comes back in.

"Oh, I'm sorry," she says off-handedly, "I thought I left my husband in here. You haven't seen him by any chance?"

"What kind of fellow is he?"

"Well, for one thing, he's an amputee."

"You're saying he stands out, is that it?"

"Not exactly."

"What's he missing?"

"His head, to start with." Jenny cocks hers to one side as she talks; her hair is done up at the back, but whisps towards the pale blue cardigan she wrapped around her shoulders before going out. She cannot help smiling at this man, though she stops herself from sitting beside him; she's had enough of being rejected in her own bed, and there's nothing she wants more, just now, than to fuck St. Julien, the pilgrimage, and the ridge, and take Stan between her legs until the sun sets through the vanes of the reconstructed windmill.

"Anything else?" Stan asks.

"You'd have to ask him."

"That would be a trifle one-sided, don't you think? ... Jenny," Stan says. "Come here," he says.

"You better get dressed if you want to meet the company in Ypres."

"You look better than the company in Ypres."

"Oh, thank you."

"Okay," Stan says, sighs, sits up, one leg akimbo beneath the bedclothes, the other reaching the floor. "You may not know this story. During the retreat here, in April of '15, when each battalion had its flanks in the air, they were trying to re-establish contact with each other, well, there was a steady stream of civilians and soldiers — gassed, stunned, terrified — clogging the road to Ypres, and there was a wounded man going back from the 15th Battalion — the 48th Highlanders, you know," Stan adds, inclusively, and Jenny nods, sits down — as far from him as possible.

"Well, this particular fellow, he wasn't walking wounded, he was in a wagon of some kind, and it was bad, whatever he had, his life was running out of him, when he saw a woman by the roadside. Do you know this story?"

"Tell it," she says.

"She was in labour. She was in labour during the first gas attack in history. And there was nobody to help her. And she couldn't have got on that wagon to save her life. And even if she could, the roads were full to bursting, the wagon couldn't stop. So this wounded man —"

"He got off the wagon, didn't he?"

"He gets off the wagon, and he delivers her child in the ditch. He wasn't a doctor or anything. So, he wraps the baby in his tunic, and hands it to her."

"And he dies." Jenny says, sharply. "He died, didn't he?"

"He did. But before that he said," Stan pauses, shakes his head like a newborn foal, "he said, 'I thank thee, sweet lady, for bringing your best beauty before my eyes shut forever.'"

"He didn't say that," Jenny says, half angrily, turning her face to the window. "The woman spoke Flemish, and he's dead anyway. We have no idea what he said."

"I know what he said, because I know what he saw, and it wasn't just a bloody baby wrapped in khaki."

Why did you have to go and *marry* him? Jenny asks herself, crossing her arms and drawing her cardigan tightly around her waist. Wasn't it enough, after twenty years, to slum it in oriental at his concert party? Dressed as a soldier dressed as a woman pretending to be a princess to a battalion of typesetters. Cleopatra among the scholars. You should have known there would be trouble in bed.

"I thank you, lady," Stan continues, "for bringing your best beauty before my eyes continually."

Bastard, she thinks.

"Liar," she says.

38

FAITH

THERE HAS NEVER been anything quaint about church.
Faith, in the face of a world before anesthetics; faith, in
the face of infant mortality, of mothers soaked in newborn
blood; faith, in the faces of the faithful themselves, was not
only difficult — it was an impossibility, and no sane person
ever gave it a second thought. Thought was not the issue.
With God, they were told, all things are possible. Faith
was serious business when so much business turned on
bafflement: wide acres of time, open oceans of space, ruled
and squared and shook out for china sets and heavy-set men
and women, who served out tremendous helpings to their
gods, and hoped for a good return.

Bargaining? Why, in heaven's handlessness, not?
Peradventure there be but five. Peradventure she should
say, no; peradventure he should be a brute in the midst of
total night? Peradventure the weather should come, stoking
from the north its mortal flares. Peradventure there should
be nothing left, and none to mourn, the farmhouse and its
outbuildings an imprint in Prairie braille, for moving fingers
of sunlight to read?

They dressed for this. Sunday best was no picnic, either. It
was the apotheosis of industry, the Word made fabric, woven
from hour to hour and from day to day. All that lies in our
power, Lord. All that, lies, and much else known, or else
feared to be so. Rake and hoe; seed and reap. And for Fred
Abercrombie, his belly his battle standard, his very spine his
shepherd's crook — straight as an arrow, bowed as only his

bared head bows, each Sunday, at the altar of all that is social
and true enough — for Fred, this was the rallying point,
his *Place d'armes*, or even forlorn hope: battle on, battle
on. Quaint got on in the Prairies like a doily in a threshing
machine. These people were serious.

"You don't need to house that," John thought out loud,
contrariwise to all I have been telling you. The Son of Man
has nowhere to lay his head.

"You know, Christ is here," Fred answered, going along the
pews, righting hymnals, straightening bibles, pairing each,
red with black; slaught, slack.

"Don't get carried away, now."

"I didn't mean you."

"You'd think I'd know," John went on, "but I gotta tell you,
I haven't seen much of anything since I went over."

"I'm not sure you have," Fred answered. "Gone over, that
is." He missed the soldier metaphor and landed right on
target. And the silence that followed was almost as scary as
if Herald really had knocked down every candle in the place.

39

HAD WANTED

HAD WANTED to go over. Wanted — some proper sort of war. Instead of. Steady. The readiness is appalling. And then — the gas rolled back. Dipping its all-toxic ink into every crevice in the well-strewn ground. Their own cloud, the thing they'd released to clear their way. Supposed to be blown uphill. You'd need a stiff wind to — and so they *ck-ka-ka-cha chat-ah-ka-pla* humped over the parapet, into the full range of the face of it, the German riflemen and machine gunners untouched and waiting. Waves of 108th men cutting up as down they went, most slumping back into the very trench where swilled with gas ... This was to have been the raid of raids, the March strike at Hill 145, before the great day proper when the ridge actually fell — what an odd locution, Stan thought, in that trauma-word way he had — fell to the Canadians, who non-figuratively fell before him, here, and kept falling, back into their jumping — God in heaven — off trench, to drown in the gas that blew back at them.

Not in the first wave, Athelstan Allward, so he could see, and saw all hopeless. Would not order 13 Platoon to go. Over they went over anyway, crying bitter mercy on those left below. Go, go, go. Would have followed after, but first one, then another, of his own wayward men, falling back on him. Gas. Had his respirator on. Boxed.

It was then that John. And hauling him up by his Sam Browne at first then into (somehow — Herald had ways of — catlike — slinking through anything: scout) a forward sap, bluishness of sky turning dawn above them and then they worked forward, from clump to claw and clawing clear they went. This was 4th Division stuff and nonsense had to prove themselves twice over: not just Canadians but the new division, the last of the rump of the ground littered with body parts of a world never before parlayed into chalk. Forward. So that they even came to. Bombs. Rifle grenadiers. Cleared (what a word for what a trench looked like, bombarded and captured!) a half-mile of Fritz coming back at them now, cut off, holding the rim of nothing ventured nothing.

The officers remained. At first sending back the men. Shot in the — now that word was everywhere you looked. Blown, fallen, worked. Back. And then John turned to him. Your turn, Mister; yours but not your time: Stan read it as clear in his eyes as I am talking to you now. Impossible. Not your time, or mine.

How did any of them? The gas blown back and beyond recall, had gone over anyway and now his hands shook like poplar leaves in a gale. Had to hide them behind his. Wrung it out of him, the Colonel did, the Old Man pale, sheeted, dead. Scattered where they fell. From his hands and now, with the battalion history stacked about him, in front of Union Station, Arthur Ernest Leading waited for devil-may-come-all.

40

VOICE US

The ground went up before us as we walked,
combusting onward, stride for measured stride,
gliding up the incline rendered rude
by the pockmarks of infanticide:
earth's children turned prodigal, monstrous, balked
at nothing but our mother's open, wide
mawkishness. Come to me, all ye that stalked
at night the triple lights of counter fire:
red, green, and white: blood, life, and sepulchre
transubstantiated from our footprints here
to tip the balance of obscene desire:
we were too keen by far to enter her,
so hurled ourselves into the raging, sheer —

MY GOD, STAN THOUGHT; what on earth am I going to do
with *that*?

He looked up from his notebook at the Grande Place,
aswirl with veterans, locals, and cut stone, piled up against
the new Cloth Hall that rose again — the entire city, really,
an Atlantis that had sunk beneath the weight of shells,
humming now with hope and peace.

"There is no fourteenth line."

And there he was, standing just behind Stan at his little
round table, one of dozens that spilled into the light of the
Place like so many mother-of-pearl balloons.

"Y-yes," Stan stammered, caught off guard. "I am one line
short a sonnet, Padre," Stan said, at a loss for words. *Abba,*

Father would have been more appropriate. Oh, we forget how dear he was to them! In a war that was almost as hard on established religion as it was on those who would never be re-established with anything, Canon Frederick George Scott (we'll call him the Canon after this; they did) pitched his revivalist tent as close to the Front as possible. The man who passed out cigarettes in place of bibles, who slept on front-line fire-steps with no more warmth than winter could afford; who, when challenged by sentries in the night would give the password, "German spy."

This, the hawk-nosed Padre who, in 1919, sped to minister (read: rally) the general strikers in Winnipeg (his Quebec Diocese yanked him back like a dog in heat), the author of *The Great War as I Saw It* and — perhaps most importantly for this story — the only Canadian author to whom Stan had sent, or would ever send, his own efforts, hovered over him like an old crow. Stan stood up sharply when the Canon clawed his cane, leaning forward to get some leverage on weary limbs.

"You don't mind if I have a dekko, do you?" Stan whisked an extra chair, quick as a rifle clip, for the Canon to sit on, made a gesture at once gracious and awkward, and then there was a pause during which Stan watched a little dog, tethered to the back of a wagon-load of stone, try to make momentary contact with every man, woman, and child within a dozen yards of its attendant trajectory.

"What's the story?" the Canon asked, as he read the poem.

"Well, Padre, you see, right there, that's the problem. I'm supposed to complete the Colonel's regimental history, but I keep having the same dream. I've done the research, and I am holding the battalion history, finished, in my hands. It is precisely one thousand pages long, although, to look at it, it's no bigger than *The Great War as I Saw It*. Every time I open it, the contents have shifted, whole sections are blank; I check the contents page—gone—try the indices—numbers wrong. I shut and open it like a shutter light, trying to catch the contents as they vanish. And each time I open the book, it gets a little shabbier: half-torn pages hanging by a thread, entire signatures ripped out, and sheaves of orders stuffed in the gaps. I mean the actual orders, scribbled under fire, start falling from between the changing pages. It's usually about then when I realize: one thousand pages, one thousand men. But six times that number actually pass through those boards—cling, momentarily, to that leathern spine, before being torn out. Six thousand Canadian men telling their story in one thousand voices, all at once, with those very voices rising and falling and fading away. A shell game. From hell. No one remembers anything. There is no battalion history."

"No one remembers everything, Athelstan." Stan started at hearing the Canon address him by his full, first name. "You have been very hard on yourself. Wasn't the war enough for you? You can only tell the story as you saw—or rather, experienced—it. That's what we want to hear. You tell your story aright, the history will take care of itself."

"But say one of the Originals wants to remember—"

"The Originals are about as busy as Satan in a seminary trying to forget just what their last engagement was actually like. Go on, son. You survived them. Their only hope of voicing lies with you: your voice."

The Canon paused, then said, "Voices." Paused again. "Voice us," he said at last, and turned the notebook page.

41

MISSING

"DADDY?"

"Lucy."

"What does this say?"

"It says, A SOLDIER OF THE GREAT WAR."

"Who is it?"

"We don't know. Nobody knows."

"Why?"

"Well, because, in war, when you're fighting, you don't always have time to stop and bury the dead."

"Can't you tell who they are?"

"Not always."

"Why?"

"Not always."

"Were you ever dead?"

"No, honey, not yet."

"What does this say? Daddy? What does this say?"

"It says, KNOWN UNTO GOD."

"God knows who's here."

"Yes, God only knows."

"How many people does God know?"

"God only knows, honey."

"Some of these have rocks on them!"

"Yes, don't touch them, Loosey-Goose; leave them there."

"These are all the same."

"They're all the same, but they stand for someone different, underneath."

"Are you different, underneath?"

"Your mother thinks so."

"Mommy doesn't know. Daddy? Mommy doesn't know."

"Let's go honey; I can't find who I'm looking for anyway."

"Da-dee. There's no one here."

"Go find your mother, sweetheart, back in the bus there. Go on."

So Art found the markers of the dead in his platoon.

42

THE SKY WAS NOT OUR OWN

JOHN SITS at the dining room table, the room aslant with sun. She sees him from the kitchen, half his back to her, face bent over a newspaper, parsing out the words. Slow.

"What are you doing, Johnny?"

"Getting caught up."

"Don't you know already?"

"No, not really."

"Can you make out the words?"

"Is that why you became a teacher?"

"I had to do something."

"Because I didn't write."

"I had to do something, Johnny." And what on earth is she going to do with him now? Chores?

"I was wondering …"

"Yes?" She stands in the jamb, wiping her hands on a dish-rag, wringing the rag around her knuckles, wringing, then unwringing; rewring, unwring, wrung.

"I'd kind of like to write to you, now."

"Now?"

"Yes."

"Why?"

"To leave something behind."

"Besides me, you mean."

"Beside you, yes."

She'd almost forgotten how particular he could be, with words, which he heard as keenly as he sensed everything else, for all his trouble with the alphabet.

"Do you want me to write for you?"

"Kind of."

Mary Helen's hand fitted over his. This isn't going to work. And then he was in her head, his voice in her mind, and hand—they were really and truly, hand in hand. *Write.*

Yesterday, we went over. You couldn't hear to speak. I think this nation now. It snowed. There was sun.

Tell me more.

The sky was not our own. It was like loud toffee. The ground shook out its dead.

More.

Later, much later, when we went again. I saw her whom my soul loveth. Rose. Then, briars.

Who, Johnny? Without a trace of.

Fell among thorns. They snapped her back.

A knock on the porch door. She looked towards the sound, then back to John.

"I'd better get that."

It was Fred Abercrombie. It was Sunday afternoon. It was so bright outside she blinked beneath the hand she put to her forehead, like a salute. How are you, noticed you weren't at church, expecting nothing. But she invited him in, as she often did, only, this time, it was just to see. Fred took off his hat, keeping it in his hand, and wiped his shoes on the mat, then went into the hallway, and right on through the dining room to the sunlit kitchen, where they always sat, when he came to visit. He put his hat brim down on the table, his hands on his knees, and beamed his big man's grin, his face an apple she would never bite.

And it was as she had expected: there were newspapers on the dining room table, and sun on those newspapers, but not so much as a single strand of blonde, anywhere.

43

TRENCH QUARTER

STAN BUMPED THE DOOR with his backside. The key fell
out from the lock opposite.

He listened, a man on post, for slightest hint of —.
She did not stir. Oh, the island that they now were! By
the spring of 1918, the traumas of trench routine were
engrained for life. Only here, on what Stan called the rue
de Rimbaud in the Trench Quarter (it was, in truth the
rue de Buci, on which the poet — *dit le grand véritable* by
Athelstan — had once, briefly, stayed), during this — the
only holiday of their entire officered lives, could Stan
still — or was it that the all-go-rhythmic curves of her
could still undo the shaking, sweat-stained beggary that
was right on top of them, most midnight hours, always,
already? So, instead of breaking into a white sweat, what
time the clarion cans beyond the wire had sounded the
tocsin for an entire night of counter-attacks and reprisals
(replace the key falling from the warded lock with a pin
snitched from the Mills bomb he threw right into an
oncoming face, blowing the features over the flare-lit earth
like choice cuts from the *Bucheron de guerre*), Stan thought
and thought only of her star-splayed hand on the door latch.
That little hand (they weren't that little) had fed him, last
night, the last flan they had bolted down as an aperitif for
sleep.

"What's that?" he had asked, knowing fully what is was:
fuel for that figure eight of sex they skin-skated each night
under the bedclothes — a thresher, or steam bindery, beating

out or bringing together countless virgin harvests from the barely laundered fields —

"*Ça,*" she said, in her best Bell Frank — the nickname they had given to their version of bastard French — "*Sah ... say la heb doh ma dairy coo avant de la nuit.*" She paused for effect, then took it from her open mouth — trailing a line of slobber like the vine handrail of a swinging bridge — and popped it in his.

"It's a local expression," she continued, splashing in fatuousness. "France, you see, was once ruled by a succession of dairy cows — either the country was or the calendar — or both. It had to do with their use of — you know — Louis Cans to store their milk in. They stored it by the moon. Yes! You know how important alnamacs — hey, mister, eyes ... *front!*" (Stan's had wandered past the bedclothes scarfing her down like an amorous python) —

"Almanacs," Stan began to cor-

"You see, right there — that's the difference between us. You were thinking, she's just making this up, like this bed we haven't made for more than — stop that! Oh, no, don't stop altogether. Just that — anyway, you were thinking —"

For an instant of something not here in front of me, Stan thought. How on earth did they get her this far? The authorities, the war, nay, time and space itself, concentred here: her? He was thinking of the Front, but not now, with his backside resting against the door, and an entire —

Well, how he had got it upstairs was one thing. "Mais, monsieur, vous ne pouvez pas ..." haul this confectioner's catastrophe up the *ass-en-sir*. And so, Sir Allward found himself backing ass forward up four flights of servants' stairs, waddling it backwards down the narrow *sous-les-toits* corridor to ... *je t'adore, adorer la cœur, la sœur d'or* ... you get the idea. He was crazy with things to bring her, with this one tonic: nothing he lavished on her (either on the other side of these locked slats of kindling or out there, on the wet spring streets, literally dripping with the stars that blinked at them from *petite trues de roo*), I say not one of the hats, wraps, flowers, books, scarves, postcards, flowers, cloaks, knickknacks, flowers, bijoux, furniture covers, flowers that he lavished on her would make it back to the Front. She left them all, in the room, when they left for the last time. She didn't have to tell him.

He already knew. How many privates' haversacks had he despoiled of war booty and souvenirs in the very pith of action? He felt, now, as if he had discovered the key to providence: improvidence. That, and the very meaning of money. There was no help for it. He fairly banged the door with his butt, and when, at last, her sleep-slugged form rose and opened it, What-the-fuck-is-that never got past her kiss-missed lips. Instead, it was, How did they do the ... and, What was a nursing sister doing in a ... and, Are those tracks really edible?

It was a wedding cake, shaped like a Mark V tank.

44

LOSS IS SOMETHING

"That's not your hand," Fred said.

"What?"

"On the paper, at the table. That's not your handwriting. Who was here?"

The thing about Fred was, he wasn't asking the question in the way just about any other man — or woman, for that matter — would ask it. He genuinely wanted to know, for the sake of knowing; he had the curiosity of a cat crossed with a prospector. Days when he could rest from his work on the farm, he spent entirely in making the rounds of the square parcels of land from Carman to Roland and Morden and beyond. He sat, in his buggy (and, later, his car), in the throughways of those he knew well, by the roadsides of others, and just stared. He didn't visit unless you marched right out the front door and asked him in. He was busy with machinery and outbuildings, with who had what: binders and reapers, mowers and rakes, disc harrows, drag harrows, disc drills, and cultivators; how neatly kept; shelter belts and gardens; how many head, how many hands; how many acres, per bushel, per man. And it was a man's hand he had seen, passing through the dining room into the sun-bright warm.

"Would you be satisfied with something less than the truth?" she asked.

"No, I don't suppose I would."

"Well then, that's Johnny's hand there, Fred," she said, and sighed, and looked him straight in the eye. "John Herald," she added, needlessly. "His hand."

"Is he here, now?"

"I don't know. He was. Just before you came. He comes and goes. I'm not crazy."

"I didn't suppose you were."

"I don't know. I know it can't be him. He's not lying to me," he's lying with me, she thought, on the sly, but she was angry, and not just with Fred.

"Did you ever wish something were true, and then it happened, and you didn't want it anymore?"

"Well now, let's see. I once wished that the Halloway boy would come to trouble; he used to beat on me at school. Later, when he got his hand caught in the thresher, his whole arm … it took me a while to clear my conscience of that. So yes, I guess I have."

"Well, I want this, and I don't, and I do, and I don't, and I do. Does that make any sense to you? Because I know you don't believe me — you, the biggest believer I've ever met. And you don't want me to have this. I can feel it."

"I want what's best for you."

"Johnny told you to look out for me."

"Yes, he did."

"Then look out, Fred, because he's here."

She'd never spoken to him this way — never spoken to anyone, this way: sharp and short and bristling. She knew she was being childish and she knew she was going to lose, but what loss could be greater than the one she already had?

Fred just looked at her.

"You see," she said, at first formally, by way of an upright apology, "you see, Frederick Abercrombie, loss is something I *have. Don't take that away from me.*"

And he got up to go.

45

DON'T

Toronto, 1918

SPEAK FOR ME HERE. My dear.

Because she has appetite and is not afraid to show it.
Because she'll eat anything, provided you can grow it.
Because she can't sweat in the sun.

Loves mud, my darling one! Cools her down; coats her, too. There are so many things I would have liked to show you.

Because she makes a ruckus, not a mess; because we kill as often as we bless.

And because there is no cause for her happiness.

I was a born raider of gardens, a Satanette with a penchant for hand-me-downs. Handle me, don't mangle me. This town, this city, throve by slaughter, at last has Flavella, her very own daughter. Killed before they went to Troy. Nothing funny about that.

Can't tell you of the time they came to take her. Will, later. Because her nose is not cute. Because she squeals loud and long. Because we name her with the very brutes. And because she roots, and roots, and roots.

Look at the two of you—hark your angel Herald sings—covered in mud, and the strength that soil gives. Rare in a city as dirty-poor as this one, coal-shot down a thousand cellar doors. We are at the parting of ways; there will be other Torontos, but none that know my earliest days. My earliest, my ears are wet with expectation.

Flow on, Flavella, you Queen of Pignation!

Thought I'd throw a little Whitman in there, just to be sure you're listening. You are, aren't you, dear? Stuck in a sap, with your ears to the ground, waiting for, wanting nor, don't make a sound! She'll squeal anyway. She'll rend the heavens with howls of, Oh, is this *the* Garden, really with green, and orange, at night, and aglow?

46

SANDBAGS OUT OF STONE

THEY'VE MADE THE SANDBAGS out of *stone*, Stan thought, the same way you might say, Oh, you *shouldn't have*, to some much-wanted embodiment of the ephemeral, flowers of the forest of seedlings that pushed and pined in their hearts, the Pilgrims, come at last beneath the shadow of those pylons that heaped their eyeless angels into sky.

Concrete sandbags, blanched bricks, petrified pillows, the exact opposite of what they had been: cushions to absorb the shock of shells. Stan's eyes bounced off them in the bright, so pulled out his shades and put them on, then let himself into the trench, slipping down heel-scuffing sides and landing in a farmer's squat, on the stolid, unsinkable ... bath-mat, high and dry as a martini raised to erase the past. This was Vimy; this, the Canadian front line. Make it last.

Is this what would have happened if the war had gone on? Say 1936 marked its 22nd year: stone sandbags, fixed positions, civilization perpetually under siege? And what's the difference, he thought, in a million years some benign hand will unearth this park of Armageddon and trace the lines of primeval war. Stan had married Jenny and with her had re-entered time and space—and he was aging rapidly. Soldiers' heart had come with that heart of hers, his heart of stone gave way to sand—he couldn't shore it up—running through the hour-glass of passion.

That ran out here: clambered over these steeps of stone, the lees of courage left behind in the deafening overshot. Overran, he remembered, the dazed Germans coming up after the first wave had passed them by. Some had fought; some surrendered; some were shot as they wondered, or taken as they thought.

The night before, Stan had dreamt of shells coming right for his head: had felt their metal spiralling towards him, heard the whoosh of their velocities, and felt, too, sheer helplessness, not elation, as he had here, before. He couldn't believe he'd survived it, Hill 145 — his mother, he recalled, striding over broken rugged riven, beside him, sudden, stepping through the terrain of her Miltonic mind. What did she quote? Leviathan. Petrified. Stone boat; concrete sea, their struggle for the fixed in the flux of muck cast into pure form. Nobody, nobody is hurting me.

Vimy was unique in that it forbade defence in depth: its sheerer side facing east, its delusively easy slope west, lap of death that had drowned a city of Moroccans thirsting with knives, preferring their bayonets to bullets, dodging nothing. It was defence in height alone, raised, like these walls of stone, that Stan's hands stroked now, stroked now.

Jenny smiled down at him, standing on the parados, and made to go, leave him with his memories, but he wanted her beside him. Come down; come on. These stone sandbags — he wanted her soft beside him. When they had given, he had not; his hardened body had brushed their corners raw. He wanted the strength of her beside him now, that swaying gait of the first felt love of his life. She smirked down at him, sensing him, wanting her, straining upward like a boy in a bathtub.

Let him wait, she thought. I'm not going to be groped, even by you, my darling, before the King arrives.

47

PRESENT

GONE, FAR GONE, missing on the other side of yesterday.
As we grow older, time telescopes and what was untold
leagues away speaks almost among us—in the next room, in
the corner of the loose-striven field, or across the water, if
only we can again set forth. This day, we Canadians, *nous, les
canadiennes*, are four thousand, plus representative swarms
from the two nations that fought each other (for centuries, and
nothing won) to become us and for whom we, in turn, fought:
overseas, in and for France; overseas, for and from England.

Canada, fathered on the ridge at Vimy, an esker
scraped by rawhide slaughter; mothered, too, by German
militarism—this hump on the rude nub of the Western
Front. A present, to Canada, from France. French soil.
Canadian toil. Here, take it.

King Edward, at ease among the vets, mingled freely,
extending that hand from across the sea that Britain still had,
armoured by dreadnoughts racing to be out of date. The
infantile fantasy of transnational paternity—the mottled
elixir of the mother country, made, briefly, young again by
this compassionate King, who then addressed the gathering:

"All over the world there are battlefields, the names of
which are written indelibly on the pages of our troubled
human story."

Human story. Stan liked that. Not history. Troubled will
do. What's indelible? Twenty years? Twenty seconds in an
exploded mine, suffocating, on gas, underground? Indelible
to whom? The man is dead.

The King went on, his loud-spoken syllables trip, drippingly, under an overcast sky. "It is one of the consolations which time brings that the deeds of valour done on those battlefields long survive the quarrels which drove the opposing hosts to conflict. Vimy will be one such name."

It was the 26th of July, 1936. Time brings many things, Stan answered, but I don't think consolation is one of them. Jenny shushed him. Had he spoken out loud? In vain he searched for traces of *guillemets* — always a giveaway — fading in the Artois air.

"The masterpiece which rises before our eyes, by its grandiose dimensions, its proud and pure symbolism, is one of the most remarkable among the many which commemorate, on the field of battle, the valour and abnegation of warriors."

Valour and abnegation — not bad, Stan concedes, for someone who wasn't there, as they were then, and are here, now, nineteen years after, on the flip side of the gentle slope that shore their lives in two, grinding their sinews apart by craters blown at dawn or reliving, dead or dead to the world, the world, at war, that was.

"See, at the top of those two pylons — representing the Canadian and French armies — " Jenny cranes her head, but loses the statues, just stares into indifferent blue. Drone on, young ones; drone on by, low-flying fighter planes. Was this what they left Canada for, first in 1914, and now, in 1936? To look up while the past droned interminably on, into the present, which hardly anyone knew?

"... peace, justice, honour and loyalty for which they fought, sending up to them a triumphal hymn ..." Sending up to them a bi-assed donkey, Bill thinks, its twin fundamentals piling on and on. He stands with Art, his old comrade, just behind Stan and Jenny, to the right. Look up, Canada. But Bill looks down, at Stan and Jenny's right and left respective hands, spliced together like frozen cordage. Nothing new there; the old Lewis-gunner is used to moving parts that fit in the dark (trained, as they were, to dis- and reassemble their weapons blindfolded). *Do not talk too much about things that cannot be seen.*

Spent so much fucking time inside these things you never want to know about it as imagine trying to walk-aim-fire while sacked inside of black rubber these steamed-over portholes for eyes of your either-sided head like a river horse or dragonfly monster; if you take it off you're fucked if you leave it on you're blind enough to run for air not long under khaki-wrapped body-sausage your own fat slicking down your sides and ready to be stuck.

That's one sentence if you want more follow me over this lip of shit-stained up-gut of earth one step you're dead two you're dead right: respirators at the heady murder, boxed before your toxic nostrils not unlike the arrow-clouds at Agincourt barely heard or seen gas shells plonk in urine soaked with dirt. It takes more than to give and there's no giving way just taking to take more take more and less what is left: pure hate for such a body that could make and manufacture this deliver us from evil smells but in what tarnished hells of über-struggle would order forward in the face of no face?

The *Field Service Pocket Book* never said nothing about this you cunt fuck fuck fuck can you believe firing from the slung over shoulder strap hip soldiers do fuck fuck fuck fuck fuck this kind of fuck every fucking thing fuck time. To stay alive. Just to. Stay.

Grow Beautiful Hair Free!

Bill had donned his box respirator as the second yellow-green cloud, scarce released, began to slow, then blow, slowly, back—a livid nightmare deciding, *après tout*, to be true—not because he wanted to live but because he didn't want to die like *that*: man-made hacking flesh out of stone cold dead for days after sometimes years later or just a forced march away, away from the fighting God help me lift this death-rattling soul-splitter spitting runts from the literally dead ground and Fritz on the *qui vive*, bayonets on Mauser-mawed sparklers like fireflies gathered from the fields at dusk at breeze for a breath of and sure enough some did rip the masks in red-faced fury at nothing but gas officers in particular in order to give way give fire give orders no one could heal after this it just sits inside you like an inverse hair-shirt lung-lined for discomfort.

Harlene?

"... while at their feet, the Angel of Victory holds aloft in the supreme spirit the flame of sacrifice." Sacrifice, Art thought. Now, there's a word for you. Not a fight. Not even resistance. What soldier worth his salt had any use for it? His Majesty's Canadian Sacrifices—a ship of fools. The former sergeant of the 108th (Toronto Typographic) Battalion, C.E.F., had thought that one up on the voyage overseas—the third time he'd crossed the Atlantic and, strange to say, the first time he was scared.

"Here the veiled virgin, a touching image of the faraway land, devoutly weeps"—and Stan started right in, as if on cue—"weeps over the tomb where, under helmet and laurel, the host of sacrificed warriors sleeps its last sleep."

Fine and dandy. If you but knew how few of those gathered below you had any notion left of what sleep was. They dreamt of slumber the way syphilitics dream of puberty. The silken Union Jack that had tarped the (in- no-way-virginal) figure of Canada Mourning Her Dead lay swaddled, arterial bunting at her stone feet. When the sun — at last — broke, momentarily, through the clouds, her lidless eyes burned like trench flares in a moonscape of stare.

48

AND STAN WROTE

Stand for Canada

When I first saw you, standing there, alone,
I knew you were the answer to a question
in the form of another question, Why are
you here? Not how. This is one of those moments

when why is what you have to know, and make
known. And Allward carved at one remove
and made you out of roaming all the earth
a place to stand and rise from yourself.

I am here to remember what cannot be
recalled; I am here to mourn, in these fields,
and be proud. Two things we need, spirits or
no. You do not say yes or no or know
why. Those eyes! Those eyes! Know why. No why.

49

UP, UP

"Okay, you go back, now," Sapphira says, and hands Alley the torch. The latter keeps her arms by her sides. The two girls stand ankle-deep in the freezing run-off; the light from Alley's storm lantern flickers the yellow brick, gold; their serried order holds firm in this sink of fear. Alley's eyes go glazing like those thousand-year-old figures fired to guard the Emperor: brick battalions — upright, patient, resistless, and fatal — warding off, with so glazed a gaze, danger; their burnt-in duty — blind to mind — the foundation of all loyalty.

Horseshoes ladder up and away from the vaulted nether creek — they have reached the feeder that runs from the abattoir — and the horseshoes ascend this barrel of stone, twister of conveyance aimed at the underfloor of offal. Understore of awful, Alley varies, playing with words to keep from thinking, her eyes blinking in the torchlight.

"Okay," she says, and moves a muscle somewhere out of sight, but not for walking.

"So, take it. *Take* it," Sap adds, with emphasis, trying to be cruel.

"Only," Alley adds, her arms still motionless, mousy hair sprouting from her uprooting toque, "only, I'll tell you my name, my real, full, first name, if you let me go with you."

"So, tell me," Sap says, fully intending to leave her there, to send her back, safe; intending, in fact, such a whack of verbal and (if necessary) physical cruelty as to put paid to their friendship forever.

"After," Alley adds — and knows full well. She's seen Sapphira in a fight, and not just for her — kicking crotches, tearing hair, scraping faces raw. And she's expecting one, now, when something shrugs up the tunnel, a little wave laps at their freezing feet, and a dull, hollow roar almost begins to, no — most definitely grows from the tunnel they —

"Ah-hhh — " Sap draws in her breath to find she has none, can't even speak what both girls and several rats (cast in non-supporting holes) know. Somehow, in this prince of winters, it has rained while they've journeyed underground, and when it rains, the creeks of Toronto, hooded and brick-shod, fill up — in seconds, like shotguns — to blast their barrelled passages bayward through sewers rifled with pointing.

The girls missed the warm front blowing in; the Triton-spiked lightning and the sudden squall over the bay, thinning the crust of ice between industry and islands. They have missed everything — the changes of life in a world at peace, the chance to grow up in the Gibson Girl idyll of their adolescence — but not this swipe of fate, which bounds to thunder: a wall of water under pressure from ten thousand tons of Toronto. Sap drops the torch and throws Alley against the horseshoes.

"Up! Up!" Sap shouts, and her friend — cut to the forehead by one rung and kneed by a lower one — climbs so fast she cuts her fingers through her mittens, hands and feet missing some rungs, tearing others from the mortar, screaming, "I'm missing one! I'm missing one!" which Sap neither hears nor heeds as she hasps the horse handles, half her body caught in the daggers-drawn waterblast, thick with icicles knocked from the sewer-vault.

Her left foot reaches the first shoe to hold after Alley's escalade and hauls her coat up sopping from the turgid dark — there's no black like this; what's dark when there's no light? It's just *un*. Alley howls now, shrieks down and up (the rushing water, ten times ten times louder, silences her as effectively as a box barrage) — *Say something say something say something say*— she thinks she's buried her friend in her mistakes, the rungs she's wrung from the convex wall.

Sap's answer, which cannot be translated, is something between an alley-alley-in and a struck animal, but her friend hears it, hears and, what's more, understands, as if Sapphira were standing beside her in the quiet of a winter's night, "I'm still here, you sweet fucker; keep going and don't get in my way."

Did young women swear in wartime Toronto? Did Sap want to sound like her borne-away brother? Do pigs squeal when they're slit up the middle to bleed out their lives on the slaughterhouse floor? Do men's bowels give way as they go over, wading through the same stuff they're shedding? Does anything, really, happen in literature that occurs in the world?

Their coats dripping, the girls paused above the sluicing torrent, Sap's face buried in lower folds of Alley's wet, green shade, one leg on, the other dangling, both arms around Alley's waist, gripping the shoe that dug into her friend's back. The more she hugs her, the more it hurts, but never a boo do we hear from Alley-Who.

Arterial refuse, Alley thinks, to distract herself. Well, at least it's got the word, art, in it, Sapphira answers, without speaking.

"Artemisia?"

"Nope."

"Alligator?"

"I hope not."

"All's clear?"

"Yep."

And so they clambered on, while the distant chambers expulsed their fulsome contents as far as Lighthouse Bay.

50

SO VERY SORRY

"Okay," Lois says, after everyone's settled behind their second drink and the small talk has died down, "Dream or Diary: round robin. Who wants to start?" That last she throws straight across the table, emphatically at Jenny, and of course, everyone laughs. Dream or Diary, an ice-breaker: tell about something you want to have happen, or something that has happened, since last we met. Jenny knocks her drink back.

"Dream," she says, defiantly. Lois raises an eyebrow. Jenny looks around, takes a deep breath, and then says, long-sufferingly, "I want still to fit inside my dress uniform."

"My dear," Gramm interjects, "you're not the only one with that wish."

"Not by half," Sophie adds.

"Which half?" Clare —

"I'd start with the top, for one." Flossie, holding her blouse away, looks down and up with X-Ward eyes.

A yelp or two, and then, "Top or bottom, what difference does it make?"

"Orderlies, bring the shears!"

"Which half, Lizzy?" No one calls her that but Jenny, and not in any public but this. Lo pauses. She looks at the long fingers of her left hand, propped in a vee against the glass.

"The distaff!" Ammy slams her drink on the table.

"I don't think it matters," Lo answers, quietly, "so long as you let it out."

"The fabric, or the fat?" And so on. It's Jenny's turn. She looks around the table, these faces like the phases of the moon, some waxing, some waning, but all aglow with each other's reflected company. She settles on Lois, looks her straight in the face.

"Pearl," she says.

Marjorie laughs like the rest of them — Jenny, looking at one person and saying the name of another. It was an old gag.

"Right," she says, and pushes her empty tumbler — a double shot glass showing the Horseshoe Falls (The legend? *Buck it!*) — directly at Lo, who fills it up again, directly. A few giggles more, but everyone can tell, the mood is about to shift. No one minds; this is why they are here.

"There was this boy," she begins, and everybody also knows, by the way she says *boy*, that she means a soldier — and not an officer, but an enlisted man, and almost certainly (although not necessarily), a Canadian.

"And he used to ask, every time I came on duty in the Ward, 'Did you miss us, missus?' And I'd answer, 'I'm not married, dear' — I called everyone dear, when I was on my own. It somehow made it safer — not just for me. If the patients were like family ..." and she trails off.

"There was less likelihood of their dying," Gramm says, followed by a general stir of consent.

"It just seemed good manners, somehow, to me, and they knew never to say sweetheart, or anything like that, back."

"They'd say, angel," Aggie said, correcting slightly.

"Oh yes, they all said that," several agree and when they say, "they all," something else changes. The electric current skip a pulse; the corners of the room disappear in the darker.

"So then he'd say, 'Did you miss me, at least, Sister Missy?'" Pearl continues, "and of course, he was missing ..." and she touches both her arms, and down at one side.

No one laughs, or finds it in the least bad taste. But, as
Pearl goes on — the treats she brought him; the letters
he dictated — that one especially, telling his Edmonton
sweetheart he'd found an English girl, so as not to burden
her with his body — traces of shapes emerge from the
shadows of the room, edged by that one green light, solitary
bulb among these sainted few, like an audience for lawn
bowling, illuminated late into the summer night. Those
whose lives they had saved, or lost, or lingered out to lose
at last. They do not speak of these, much, but can tell
when they enter the room, with their head wounds and
abdominals, ravines gouged out of their anatomy by shell
fragments, flesh epitomes of the Front. They are filing
in now, and all, without exception, are saying the last
intelligible thing to whichever sister saw them go:

We are sorry, so very sorry, to have troubled you in this way.
Good boys. Goodbyes. Goodbye.

51

PICK ME UP

THE PERFECT SILENCE of the Prairie dark. The almost utter
black. Summer asleep in its fields, and she and he, lying out
of doors on a blanket, questing the stars from the depths of
their eyes. He keeps the mosquitoes away. She doesn't know
how he does it. It's one of the strangest things about him.

"And how are you two getting along?" asked, at a pause in
town, fetching necessaries.

"Oh, we're just fine, thank you." She buys for one and
one half. Surely people notice. Small town people notice
everything.

"There's two things I can say about John Herald," says Jack
Loblaw, packing her dry goods in a box, "he needs less, and
has more, than any man I know."

"Oh, Jack." She looks down into her purse, open shut open
shut open.

"No, ma'am; that's on credit. You tell John I said hello."

How much do they know? Who are these people,
anyway? Does the narrowness of their lives multiply in the
infinity of skies like these? Their voices sink like topsoil
over a new grave when the subject of John comes up.
Something fresh and unaccountable, a minus to indicate
an addition to the earth. No one invites them over; no one
asks to speak to him directly.

She'd stopped attending church; she'd stopped showing
up at school. Fred made excuses for the former, and
intervened with the board for the second. For now, he could
cover for her, but even a collective illusion lifts. And it was

the Depression. She was going to have to be more inventive if she wanted to keep her little Shangri-La on the Prairie. Or more realistic, if she wanted to keep her job.

She felt, if she were gone for long, that John would disappear. Either that, or people would come looking for him. She wasn't sure, exactly, who. It was like he had a price on his head, which she was willing to pay, but she wasn't sure about the Dufferin County School District or the General Store. Not indefinitely. And John was, if anything, indefinite. Even lying there on the blanket, in the dark, how could she be sure he was ever really there?

"Could you pick me up?" she asked.

"Could I *what*?"

"Pick me up. I mean physically, lift me. Off the ground."

"You know I could."

"And keep me there? Could you pick me up and carry me into the house?"

"I thought you liked it out here."

"I do. Answer the question."

John sighed. "Emaiche!" he said.

"Y-" and before she got to the "es" she was hauled up by her arms and swung like a jitterbug, whooping and screaming, a girl of five. But it didn't end there. He slung her over his shoulder like a jointed feed bag and the ground flapped and flummoxed beneath her bobbing upside-down head while she kicked and squealed.

"Can I pick you *up*?" he said, thoroughly, not really asking the question. "You want *up*? I'll show you UP," and he unfolded her upright, sidewise on the saddle before she knew the horse was even there.

"Blaze," she whispered, in muffled awe. The horse's head turned ever so slightly, flicked an ear to show she knew.

Then he was beside her, Mary Helen in front, her two knees arrowed forward, her arms ivyed in his. She didn't look. She didn't want to see the shell.

"Johnny—"

And then they were off. Once out of the yard, Blaze rose under them like a wave, over the fence and into the fields. Mary Helen heard the wind where before there had been none; felt the ground shudder its staccato through the unshod hooves; felt John lean into the beast, intent on something, and then she heard the long, moaning *"waaaaaaaar, waaaaaaaar, war, waaaaaaaar"* of a steam whistle and realized, they were racing a train, converging on its blustering thudder as it sounded out a level crossing up ahead. A jump drum onto black macadam, another jump, and they were near enough to smell the cinders.

She opened her eyes. It was like riding in the clouds, Blaze a blur of grey, wake of mane in the wine-dark air, the steam from the engine making one, long, cometing ghost that poured like ectoplasm from the guttering funnel.

"Don't let go!" he shouted. The words fly past her like spray. "Hold on!" he shouted and then they must have hit another fence—how on earth did he see these things?—when Blaze jumped again only, this time, she didn't land on the other side.

52

OH, *HER*

"THERE ARE SUBTLETIES in everything," Allward said, a little in his cups, a bit overdrawn, with Jenny sitting beside him and Art and Bill across — that is to say, Art across from Jenny, Bill facing Stan — and each pair shared a small, round table, grouped beneath the awning of the busy brasserie.

"You mean subalterns, surely," Art corrected. They had nothing to talk about, at present. The bus had just dropped them off and they were still too stunned to speak: Ypres was back.

They had never known it in anything other than an advanced state of ruination. And then there was the gate, the Menin Gate, monument to the missing — "The Empire's Most Impressive War Memorial." Completed in the fall of 1927, its 20,000 tons of concrete, brick, and stone drew more pilgrims than any other lode of loss, and former Corporal Bill Ostic; Sergeant Art Cane, M.M.; Lieutenant Stan Allward, C. de G. (Croix de guerre); and Sister Jenny Gray, R.U.O.K., wanted absolutely nothing to do with it. There were lots of Canadian names on the Menin Gate, but it was an imperial monument to a remorseless zone that knew no victory. Even Passchendaele, taken, at last, by the Canadians, in November of 1917, had felt like a defeat.

As establishments went, in Ypres, this one — *Le Plus Beau du Bien* — was just a tad upscale, off the beaten track, not giving onto the Grande Place but a side road that none of them could quite remember what it hadn't looked like as the war progressively flattened and pitted the town. Ypres, the Clotho of Europe, birthplace of modern infantry (wearing scarlet coats, no less), and now, this latest revelation, from Bill's ever-expanding word hoard:

"Tell me the etymology of diapers," he said, and gave Jenny a sideways smile before settling his eyes on Stan.

"Dia ... through ... something," he began.

"De Ypres!" Bill trumpeted. "The special cotton pattern originated here. *Dye apray,*" he continued. *Die après.*

Jenny felt ready for anything; they had all had two too many and were stranded on their separate islands of unreclaimability, but Stan surprised her.

"*My little gas alarm*—that's what I call her, who has breath, at night, that would raise a gas alarm."

There was a pause, while Bill looked at Stan as if he were an idiot and Art, as if his friend was in real trouble. Jenny was raising hackles the size of peacock feathers. Art leaned across and, touching her hand to get her to attention, asked, apropos of nothing, Did she remember the girl who appeared on the Bathurst Street Bridge, that night after the Concert Party in Toronto?

"Who—*what* girl?" Stan asked, breaking in. "You never told me about a girl."

"No?" Jenny bantered back. "That wasn't all we found. We were looking for you, remember? It seems to me we are always doing that, looking for a little boy who very much wants to be found, but not by me." She stood up, knocked the table—Art caught it—and over went her half-empty third beer.

"No, no, no," she said, as if the three men were orderlies. "You are all staying right here." She gave Stan, nothing. She was gone.

"Well, Lieutenant ..." Bill began, the ellipsis almost audible in the tapping of his hobnails against the cobblestones.

"What's eating you, Mate?" Art asked more sympathetically.

Jenny complicated things. Bill worshipped her, of course; he had that through-line of adoration all the way from 1918, when she'd tended to him after the Battle of Amiens, to the Wheat Sheaf Tavern, in downtown Toronto, that night they'd met two years ago to get her onstage, opposite Stan.

"Who are those two in the corner?" she had asked, and raised the hair on the back of his head.

"What couple?" he had said—then, fully aware that he was, and she must have been, staring at the back of John Herald, dead those 18 years. He couldn't make out the girl.

"She was swaddled in black," Art said, more to himself than the others, who had not been there. "As if some rag-picker had turned to fancy dress."

"Oh, *her*," Bill rejoined. "I saw her in the Sheaf the day before. She was with a soldier. Blonde chap."

Stan, at this point, had thrown his subtleties out the washed windows of his eyes, and called for coffee.

"She was no kid, either," Bill went on, trying to deflect attention away from Herald. "More like a young miss just this side of marriage." With *what*, he wondered.

"You may have a point there," Art confirmed. "I always get carried away by those marbles. Makes me think of children."

"Stan? You okay, Mate? Here's your coffee, drink up." Stan can't hold the cup still. He shakes like an NYD (N). They sat for a while in silence, as something like sobriety entered the riots in their minds—a place at once so sacred and profane! And nothing to do but drink beer and coffee. Stan steadied himself.

"We remember nothing," he began. Not, Did you see my sister? "Memory isn't something we have. It has us, at its pleasure, or dis-, mostly dis-, except for this: what we call memory has suffered two amputations before it passes our teeth: what actually happened has been lived as a story, and that story is one that we can tell. It's a streamlining like I'm going to streamline this fish by gutting it and scraping its fins off. There. Why don't it swim?"

"You're being too hard on yourself, and on us, as usual, Mate," Art said, who had long mastered the art of Stan's manner of talking around a topic.

"You're also assuming we give two bits and a bowl of shit for your bloody fucking history of the regiment according to its dopey impresario."

Bill took a risk, with that. He knew, since they'd fought their way free of the German lines at Amiens, just how tough and reckless Stan could be. Matched himself, for one. And then there was that—fuck, why didn't he see it coming?—that girl he was off his head about. Something about her and a horse, neither of which were anywhere near us, that day, Bill thought, remembering the tank, the rank sink of batter-clang hell, ripped open by a shaft of shell that Bill took for well-aimed angels.

He was out, standing outside the shell of tank, spitting up parts of men. And then, seeing Stan now, clearly past several limit markers, and solid Art, who would walk into hell itself and ask to see the manager; I say, looking at these two infantrymen scarce into diapers, Bill joked, melted his heart. Crazy he had been, back there, when these two made all the decisions. They were the crazies, now; incurables—the one of loss, the other of goodwill, neither of which exist in war. Loss is what war leaves behind; goodwill it simply fucks to death.

"Hey, Stan," Bill says.

Stan looks at him like a child scooped from traffic.

"Hey. Will you read to us your latest, of the history, I mean. No, I actually want to hear it. Can we have *duh-low* over here, *garson*? Yeah, me too, Mate — just bring the fucking water. And two bottles of — yeah, that's it."

And the friends drew together like three men on a match.

53

HEAVEN

TWO NAKED PIGS—why do they only seem naked when they're dead? Sapphira wondered, when quicker than blinking they were upon her, jouncing jauntily—two huge, flesh epaulets on either side of the butcher's head—two little pigs, no bigger than Flavella would be now—*is* now, *is* now, she had to keep telling herself, who had taken to haunting the sooty blood smell outside the abattoir, the still living cased in sheltered pens—sheltered from being seen as beings, she had added, with the crazy faith of the young, that words can change the world. But these two, hauled from a meat truck and hurried in front of her, disappear through the door of a Chinese laundry on Elizabeth Street, shaking their sideways heads together as if to say, we're not her; don't follow us.

Flavella had followed her home. And she had followed her, too, in a truck just like this one, the day they came to take her pet away. A mounted constable—there was no end to animals in Sap's world—and a butcher's truck pulled by a dray. The butcherman holding the reins like a noose.

Constable Jim Wardle was used to such scenes, from waifs and strays to entire families forced out of their homes—more in the Ward than anywhere else, which they weren't that far from, he thought. And then he wanted to be as far away from 56 Sullivan Street as possible.

The butcher's boy came out the front door with Flavella carpet-bagged under his arms. Sap attacked, leapt right into him—he had to drop the pig—which *bang!* the front door closed couldn't get back in so scuttled along the street more or less directly into the butcherman's sooty palms. He left two hand marks on her, but Sap was too busy breaking every rule of decorum, not to mention the law, to notice. And the boy, bless him, actually wept as he swept her hooked hands from his coat. Jim dismounts, holds his horse, Dandy, by the reins, but not that girl or even this-must-be-the-mother, who storms out on the porch before falling into the short walkway, packed earth lined with whitewashed stones, leading to the street.

Jim helps her to her feet but she clocks him with her free arm as he brings her up. Now, this is a Toronto police officer, and the year is early 1918. You raise so much as a finger and look to have it broken in two places before getting it handed back to you in the wagon. Jim demurs, and takes it.

It is almost worth the pain, Sap thinks, distinctly this time, hearing it word for word in her head — like words of command given by some unshockable N.C.O. — it is almost worth the pain to see this: Gladys, not only fighting a policeman, but above and beyond and in fact all that registers isn't who she's beating as that she and Sap are on the same side in a quarrel with common sense.

"Mother! Hit him again! Mother!" which, when Gladys hears, stops her cold, and her newfound authority in Sapphira's eyes instantly turns on its source.

"There, there, child," she says, patting Sap's shoulders of a sudden still, and then shaking with the tears that kicks and claws had kept at bay.

"You boys had best get clear," she says, matter-of-factly, not even a hint of apology, let alone fear — unless it is fear for the men's safety. The only thing Gladys fears is what this will do to her baby girl.

Who busted through the laundry door into a world of sheets and steam. Antique faces look up, blank, not unkind. Is this what heaven is like? she wonders. Laundering naked bodies, white with heat and steaming home?

54

EVERDAMNLASTING

She makes her way east, towards what was once downtown, before the straight, shabby arrow of Yonge Street drew investors west, to the streets above Union Station, fountainhead to a city best reached, even in 1935, by rail. By train, not rain on November roads sleeting black in the lightless white of the King's Highway. The lake? Was as dangerous as ever. More so than the very ocean, whose depths needed all the earth to shake them outrageous. Here, one crack of winter wind could whip Ontario's meager fathoms into waves as high and baseless as the King Edward Hotel.

That had been her first stop. It was on her way and, frankly, one of the few Toronto options she had. Her income was gone but her status—not to mention her rank—was not. The fact that she'd strung beaus like plaster pearls around her over-kissed neck, that she could still dance and drink the best of her generation under the table—be that in a restaurant or a field hospital—was almost as irrelevant as antique genocide, vanished loyalties, or that she had, once, been young. The reality of it—she is on the run, from herself—hardly enters her forthright mind. She steps over the bodies of men she may once have tended or, more likely, commanded to be tended—their feet sticking out of doorways to trip her up with one more act of mercy—as if she had never done more than sail across half the world to dance and sew. No, all she wants is to see her girls again. That and, just possibly, to feel like one herself. Sisters.

She wasn't indifferent, just wise to the ways of emergency. Men, emerging from the cast of war, needed seconds to live or die. Whether a man reached the battalion aid post, whether or not he could walk to the C.C.S., where the first sisters waited, made graves or saved more lives than were lost outright. After that, it was all smoke and mirrors. Mostly. The moments of emergency are diffident as old teeth: no one would believe the sheer amount of cooked flesh they rendered pulp for war's maw, bolted down like so many fish from the barrels that served them up. Past that mouth, the jaws of well enough to make it home generally passed them on, all that was left of them, their laceless shoes thrown into the road for luck. These men were long lost. Only their names were missing from the cenotaphs that pinned each city in Canada from sea to sea. Empty graves. As if there could be full.

Her mind was wandering. So was she. Lower Jarvis Street beckoned her with crinkled gentility, made a curtsy in straits that strained and snapped like old corset bones. Get there. Just get me to the everdamnlasting stoop on time, before I look down, she wailed within for all her discharged memories to hear, at the least of these, castaway from our blood-red hands, and stop walking on forever.

55

AT LIBERTY

Toronto, 1917

HOFFENTLICH:

There's a hole where my pig used to be. Where there was some life ballast, there is none now. This city teetering towards death. Not just of her sons overseas. Turned our backs on the bay, we did; and now we're really for it.

I may go under but will come up again, with a hatchet between my teeth. I bet you didn't think that I thought like that. Well, sometimes do. I refuse to mourn what is not dead. Yet. I refuse to turn to my affairs. There are no affairs: there is only this present, now: words to you, Piperoo; and Flavella to the open air. They took her away, in a butcher's truck — the butcher struck — and I know and I know where she is.

So I'm going under, dear brother; John Odd, Junior knows from his brothers who worked for the city before overseas took them, one, two, three. How odd is that? And he drew me a map — how to find the hole where my pig used to be, and fill it with me, my fire, and set free.

I'll take Miss All-Over-Me with me; I'll take our father's torch. I'll sneak out at night and step down from the porch. And traverse the city before it awakes. And break in and out till my revision takes.

So little to depend on, Stanson; so very, very little stays. This is a hard time; I intend to be harder. I intend to take back. I intend victory.

Sapatista

56

NIGHTMARE

"EXCEPT WHOM!" Stan shouts into Art Cane's good ear.
Good in the sense that if it could hear, it would. Much
has been written about the shear amount of ungovernable
noise produced by a First World War battle-in-progress
(on its way to becoming a battle proper, Stan comments);
for my purposes, here, I can only say what it did to my
protagonist: since he couldn't actually hear anything, he
imagined hearing the sound of voices in his head (which is
different from actually hearing voices). Sometimes, they
were like his voice — that quiet inner monologue that's
supposed to comfort us when every blessed thing has
gone to shit in a thousand shoelaces. This time, it was his
mother's — Gladys's — voice, a little scratchier than usual,
but not bad given the outside competition. Young Athelstan
was coming out of a nightmare, and she was reading — to
calm him (in truth, she was reciting, but no one will believe
me) — she was reading the passage from *Paradise Lost*
she always relied on at times like these (it was a recurrent
nightmare, and Stan had it a lot):

> *But now at last the sacred influence*
> *Of light appears, and from the walls of heaven*

Walls of heaving. There are no walls in a general
bombardment. Just slopes slipping back to flat, men clinging
to a seam in the thunder-teeming slap-dash of high explosive.
But for all that, Sergeant Cane stared at his lieutenant like

a man who trusts the raging sea. He had that preternatural calm at times like these, that unmatchable whatness about his face—What? What?—Without saying anything.

"Except whom!" Stan shouts again. "Except whom! Except whom!"

The full clause runs, "Except whom / God and good angels guard by special grace." Art and Stan are squeezed together with the survivors of the early morning gas attack on Hill 145, spilt into its crease of cover like hot lead ballasting a boat.

Stan is trying to tell himself, and his sergeant, not only that he is *having* his childhood nightmare, but that this attack, across gas-happy No Man's Land, with nowhere to go but nowhere, *is* his childhood nightmare, and that his mother is telling him to not only calm down, but to begin sending back the men in little groups, while the angels—or officers—stay behind, both guardians and guarded by that same grace they cannot, in fact, extend much further than from the shallow remainder of all they will lose anyway.

Shoots far into the bosom of dim Night

Something should be said about bosoms here, for although, strictly speaking, everybody has one, soldiers knew that only women, really, did. What's more, a great many of them (the soldiers) had never seen one (let alone the two that made the word an example of the very prudery it stood for). This was not for lack of trying, or anything like polite disinterest. Lack of social opportunity crossed with youth (for that, think 16, 17, 18, and forget the official ages of enlistment) occasioned more sublimation that a corps of Salvationists.

They thought of them—the soldiers, of bosoms—bosoms guessed at or brushed by or merely shushed—*Don't tell mother*—from sisters to nursing sisters to actual sweethearts and lady loves ... however measured or far away. They thought of them more than glory or danger or even England and her Dominions. They wanted them when they lived and, for the most part—if they still had teeth, tongues, or even mouths—wailed out for them like wolves in a firestorm when they died.

Enchanted slopes or piquant spurs to a lifetime of sacrifice, the word blurred mother and other, a distinction hardly anyone had to make in those days. They fought for them, and were shot for them, far into a bosom altogether other, closer to nature than nurture. War was a bloody weaning, a monster-toothed, self-administered, actual mastectomy of images come dripping from beauty to bestial in the scope of their baby brains, and no wet nurse in sight.

A glimmering dawn—

A knock on the door; three small ones.

"Mommy?" and then, a lower, bigger voice:

"I'm with her, mother," and both Fred Allward—the children's father—and Sapphira enter, the former somewhat dazed (it is three-ish in the morning), the latter wide-eyed and searching out roots in the soil. Or so to speak. She knows the dream her brother is having, because he has told her about it, countless times. It has two versions, an earth version and a sea version.

"This is the earth version," Sap says confidently, to no one in particular.

"How can you tell, honey?" Gladys asks, not looking away from her half-thrashing son.

"Because he's moaning, mummy; in the sea version, he wails." She's making a joke, as well as being accurate: the sea version involves whales.

In the earth version, it is almost day, and the Typos are losing men just so they can use their bodies as cover for the others—or so it seems to Colonel Arthur Ernest Leading who is, impossibly, with them. No one could stop him. He'd been in the second line, with his men, who likewise needed no order forward when they heard what was happening to the raiding party (some party; there were sixteen hundred of them, drawn from every unit in the brigade) up ahead. Art and Bill had formed part of the 108th's original raiding pool. Stan followed after, in the general back-them-up outcry that shook soldiers from the Canadian lines like ice cubes from a tray. The Colonel was, quite properly, forbidden to go forward with these. That was until the gas rolled back and, on the assumption that it would reach the Second Line (that was the Old Man's excuse—it never did reach that far), Leading took the parapet like a balance beam, followed, of course, by Major Stock, the cook, the battalion diarist, and a stray dog, Jujitsu, found by a group of Japanese Canadians serving in the 108th, who had been christened Battalion Mascot but two days before. But the main difference, to Archie Stock, was that the two-leggeds all had their box respirators on; the dog had none.

... here nature first begins

Here nature ends, so Major Archibald Stock carried the animal, lest she bound into a shell hole swilled with gas. For once, the Colonel wasn't cursing, but crossing the ground over which he had sent them, came to the flags marking the gaps in the wire.

Her farthest verge, and Chaos to retire
As from her outmost works a broken foe

"Sergeant, rifle grenades!" Stan barks, loud enough to be heard, through the shock of fighting elements, wildly aware that the raiders need to set up their own counter-barrage. Close at hand, their most unbroken foe converges from all sides but one. Discussing battalion losses. Could it be they ever did this? Afterward. With Stan at last clinging to Gladys's words as if they meant something other than radical deracination in the soil, heaped with earth stuck full of the flags of all nations. He had these as a child, then lived them, several times, during the war, lived and had them and then, had them for the rest of his livid life.

With tumult less and with less hostile din,
That Satan with less toil, and now with ease

Fear is easy. Being afraid is hard. That's how it happens so fast you can barely — and then it's gone, what self-regard you might have had, and panic routs the rest of you into perpetual sleeplessness. But to be still, in fear, under fire, when the enemy has the high ground and no end of day — that, if it isn't courage, courage isn't anything, at all. How odd that it teaches you nothing. Each time it happens, it is (if anything) worse, until the man breaks, puts his head above the crust of care. It was, of war, the most frightful that ever. Ever. There were simply no gauges for it. For engagement hardly ever meant encounter. The face of battle wore a mask—and a gas-mask at that. Those who survived it did not make a friend of fear, but loaded it with extra bombs that blew them to the moon. Fluttering down, they found their feet in craterville. Fear, that great underminer, literally undermined the entire Vimy Ridge. How odd that the only way out was to amplify it, to assume, not death, but suffering *sans cesse*, and then, whenever it wasn't, to look around you with a kind of wonderless awe.

If there is a crossing over in place, some kind of *in situ* salvation, a radical ravishment we can clamp down on, and find ourselves still breathing, reading the trench flares like vivid signatures, binding the night to our overstrained hearts, these men had it. In spades, I was going to say, although in truth, more desperate digging was generally done with helmets, their basins brimming into the chlorinated moonscape to scoop out a worm's way home.

57

PUSHED UP, SHUT

Sap, Sap, pushed up. Shut. Iron eyelid, rusted shut. Pushed up, shut.

Alley hands the poker along. Clatter and bang and still, shut down. Brace and pray; grace and pry. Sifting, shifting … only just lifting. Lever and giving and sliver and grinning and heave her and *Ho! My Lady* and *Go! My Lady* and clobbledy-*wobbledy* waw- waaw-WAAAW. Clatter and bang and Alley close behind.

Hats off.

Sap asks, "So, what is it?"

There are hides and hides, not hidden but whole bodies of them, slashed, hooked and shunting along. Squeals tear the air, muggy with ick. Looking for my pet—hey mister have you seen my—pet—somebody, some bloody, some still running, trying to get away. Nowhere. There is nowhere to hide. As if naked in a nightmare that is real; as if somehow their own bodies; as if no as if. Squeal. Man-shaped shadow-snatchers moving in to catch. Chains. Hoisted. Caught up. Alive. Spilling-on-the.

Alley remembers, later, it was as if their witnessing of this was itself so outrageous that all the screams in heaven concentred them there—their eye beams lift, their hands as swift, as Sap raises the curtain of their skirts to strike. Battle then—a meat hook certainly—fists and kicks and nothing like this. The girls grab at anything they can: blades and glaives from the waists of momentarily stupefied men. Shears like wings cutting the way through. Because human.

Because there is a way through, although not for those strung ones: sliced, open mouths.

"Allemandia."

"What?"

"*Allemandia.*"

"What?"

Allemandia, Sapphira, my sister in arms.

"I'm German. We're Germans. We all changed our names." And Sap feels the room expand to contain this extra … ally. Allied. They were the Front now, both sides gathered together around the last living, casting their arms up in horror and gasp. Stone, stained floor. Shouting. A door. Where did she?

"Okay, Mister, you open this fucking door! You open this fucking door or god help me I will hook you to hell!" A push — was there kindness? And then the light, impossible light of dingy Toronto day. Their feet again. She can see. Little clovens disparting. And then that one. That shape same but different, all the difference in the world.

This way! No! Laughter like a jugular saw, like an amputated arm, laughter cracking the whipshot dawn. The bridge humps its spans, hangs its gangplank to the bay. Come on, come on! The catcall of the sun! See, brother? I'm just like you now. I'm just—

58

BILL SAID

"WAR IS NOT CONTENTION," Bill countered, hauling his mouth away from his beer. "It hardly ever—I'd say almost *never*, comes down to two men *contending* which one is the best. What it comes down to," giving his mate a sidelong glance" (Art had begun to look disgusted), "what it comes down to is some poor blood-begotten bastard being at the corner of shit and shot-at and, stead of getting across, he gets crossed out, instead. It's murder, and murder kills a man the same as killing. When he gets home, here come his friends and family—hell, total strangers—come to greet him like the travelling hero he really is, only, not in their way, see. If the murdering didn't kill him, or kill whatever perspective he might have had on the matter, coming home will drive him right over. It's *then* that his heroism starts."

"Is that our text for today, Mate?" Art asked, staring at his dark ale like a crystal ball filled with black dice.

"No, that was yesterday's. Today's is different."

"Let's hear it."

"Ever read the citations for vee-cees on the Western Front?"

"Sure, when they printed them in the papers."

Bill fished in his haversack (like Stan, he was almost never without one, even in peacetime) and brought up a wad of old clippings from the *London Gazette*. "Here's one," he said, flattening it out on the round table. "Mullin, George Harry. Very careless at Passchendaele, October 30th, 1917. Oh, he was a Yank ... actually performed the incredible feat of taking the pillbox single-handed ... says, he rushed a snipers' post ... *destroyed* the garrison with bombs ... and, get this, crawled on top of the fucking thing and shot the two machine gunners with his revolver ... says he then rushed—"

"He survived, right?" Art asked.

"Yep."

"So maybe he was just a little careless."

Bill ignored him. Found another. "Brillant, Jean: Amiens, August 8th to the 9th, 1918. Rushed and captured a machine gun, *personally* killing two of the crew ... wounded then ... rushed straight at another nest of emma gees—fifteen fuckers of them! Captured one hundred and fifty, again personally killing five ... then he detected, it says, *detected* a field gun, firing on his men over open sights ... rushed that. Didn't make it."

"Give it here," Stan said, then read: "*Je suis fini, dit le blessé, prends charge de la compagnie, car je sais que ça sera pas long.*"

"One more," Bill said. Clarke, Leo ... Battle of the Somme ... advanced to meet twenty Germans. Emptied his revolver twice, picked up a Mauser, emptied that ... but the enemy were now on him. Wounded knee, shot that guy; Fritz had had enough, turned tail, and Clarke, bleeding profusely, picked them off and pursued them until only one was left."

Art, "Did he ..."

"Died a month later, probably from his wounds. One more. For the Corps: four divisions, four citations. This one is different. Actually, you read it, Art.

"Hall, Frederick William ... *very* careless on April 24th, 1915. Irish born. Okay, on moving up to our fire-trench—ah, there's '15 for you—"

"Fuckin' fifteen," Ostic chewed through his gasper. Not a

great year for Allied field works; good trenches make bad attackers, so the thinking went.

"Anyway," Art went on, in his best course-of-instruction manner, "the ... troops had to cross a high bank fully exposed to rifle and emma gees. Says Hall missed a member of his company twice during this relief and personally brought their wounded bodies in. That must have been during the night. But, come nine the next morning, they hear someone wailing out in No Man's Land. So Hall instantly finds two volunteers, both of whom are wounded and both of whom are rescued and dragged back, on Hall's back, alive. He makes two decisions at this point, mates." Art had put the scrap of gazette down for some time. "What are they?"

"He won't waste any more men."

"Yes ..."

"So he'll go it alone," Stan concluded.

Art nodded and continued, "The fire from the hostile positions in front and on the flanks of this point in the line was now hot and accurate, but somehow Hall makes it to the guy. Joined the wounded man ... He lay flat and squirmed himself beneath the other's helpless body. Thus he got the sufferer on his back, but in the act of raising his head, slightly, to see the way back, a sniper put a bullet in his brain."

There was a longish pause. "What was the second thing, Bill?"

"The second decision had to do with everything else in his life. He had to decide that getting these men back was worth the world."

"I thought you had no truck with medals, Mate."

"Medals, yes; it's the stories. You notice how often it comes down to one Christly pea-souper of a private on some God-forboaten piece of fuck-muck to, to ..."

157

"Make the difference between victory and defeat?" Stan volunteered.

"For the entire mothering monster of Haig's anus," Bill nodded, then carried on. "Say it's here, in the Sally Ass of Lent, and it's almost always a Maxim, and it's got every man jack of us bobbing ass-up for worms and nobody—" Bill took another slug—"they're not so much beaten as played out, and this sad sap of a sergeant, this bring-it-up-the-rear orderly room refugee regalia'd in moon mufti—"

"Jesus Christ, Bill."

"This same, honest mucker of a lamb's corporal banishment decides—and the Prince of Terror only knows why—decides … it's not so much a decision as he's up and moving under Christ's own cap-stone of sky on fire and there he stands, his fear forgotten, working the bolt of his rifle like a piston in a pump house, on top of the cunting *concrete*—you know, the pillbox—waving his arms around, cracking Mills bombs like jawbreakers—or, if he's really had it with napoodling in the udder-puddle of the great shit cow—"

Stan had never wanted to kiss a man before; but with Jenny gone in a huff and Bill *en bonne forme*, he suddenly wanted for nothing. And I shall be free to possess the truth, he said to himself, in one soul but many, many bodies.

"… with cold steel." Bill had finished; Stan missed the finale, thinking of her. He looked at Bill.

"Sure, Lieutenant," Bill said, as if Stan had given an inaudible order in No Man's Land. "Sure," he said, in that oddly deferential way he had that made you wonder what you were letting yourself in for, "I'll go find her for you. You wait here with God's gift to hobnails," glancing at Art, and he was off, as sprightly as a man of half his age who had seen none of it.

59

NEVER NOTHING

"Johnny? It's way worse than you thought."

"What?"

"It's way, way worse."

"What's worse?"

"It's so bad, I can't begin to tell you."

"Emaiche, what are you trying not to not tell me?"

Good one, she thought.

"I just thought you'd like to know, that, knowing you wouldn't come/couldn't come back to me ..." and she trailed off, looking wistfully at an empty package of Redi-Glo flush enhancer: Redi-Glo — *So you don't have to!* What the fuck was it for?

"What the fuck are you saying the fuck for? What was that *for* for, for fuck's sake?"

Oh, my. She *had* said *that*. O, well. Fuck it. "O, well ... Fuck it," she said.

"You're going back on the horse," he answered, gulfing under her like a rogue wave that sweeps only one passenger away.

"Noooooooweeeeeee! Johnny. Johnny! No! John. John A. Herald, you put me ..." Where does he really keep Blaze? In his fucking pocket, she clucked, happy with the replacement for blessed in her vocabulary. Because they were in the living room, this time, but Blaze was there, very felt but whispingly seen, like a strided doily, rippling, now under Mary Helen's thighs like one very heavy stream of water, muscled by freshets that —

"Johnny, we're going up the—ah, ha, umm ..."

"Stairs, Emaiche. We're going up the"—as Blaze's altogether unghostly armature of muscular cordage river-writhed between her legs—"blessed stairs," John added, devil may care.

Later, he asked. "So, what was so way worse?"

"Wanting anyone, anyone else, while you were away," she said now, matter-of-factly. She had planned to tease him endlessly with it. But it was simply true.

"Fidelity, among the faithful, is no more than integrity among the integral. It's no effort. It's either there, or not," she concluded, and looked at the back of her hands. Sunspots.

"You mean to say waiting for nothing is no work?"

"I mean to say nothing for something is worse than nothing at all." She was thinking of Fred, who was hardly nothing to just about anyone, but her. And even to her, he was pretty big.

"Am I—is that what I am," he asked then. "Nothing, for something?"

"No, dear," she said, a little condescending, but mainly, tears. "No, you were something else. Still. Still are. Something else for something else. But never ..."

John buried what was left of his face in her short shock of wheat-grained hair—

"Never ... nothing."

60

DUD

WHEN ART CANE got to Ypres in 1936, he kissed the ground.

"There now," he said quietly. "All better." It wasn't a question or a statement.

"Dad-dee, *ew.*"

"What's the matter, Loosey-Goose? When I was here before I kissed the ground ... more often than your mother's face at home."

"Which is saying a lot of ... something—but I'm not sure what it is." It was former Private-cum-Lance Jack Hebib (although his real name was Kevin), revelling in his new rank *like a pig in shit*, he had said, repeatedly, in 1918, until someone knocked him off the pole above a latrine. He had come to the Corps particularly raw, and keen—and was punished for it, broken down, and then reformed again, on both his and the army's terms. Both persisted in him now, a rare occurrence, by then. It had been more common during the first years of the war, among the Originals—men and women of the First Contingent, and their immediate successors. Old soldiers were, by and large, highly idiosyncratic men, who remained so, long after Mars made them one.

"Don't say that in front of my kid sister." It was Stan, savaging the country with his eyes.

"You're kidding, right?" Hebib ventured, then bit his tongue. What a stupid thing to say.

"Sorry, Mate."

Kevin was one of those invisible flywheels—complete with belt and its own source of power—that any organization as mired in the past and as free as the gas to try whatever the Sam Jake they wanted—that would win—as the British Army was. The trick was to be intelligently traditional. Or traditionally intelligent, as he liked to say.

"I only kissed the ground, once."

"When was that?" Art asks.

"When the Minnie fell among us, that day Bill fell into the sky for a while."

"It was a dud," Bill added, regretfully.

"It was a dud that just about took my leg off," Art added. "So I remember, before we got the thing out of there, I kissed its muddy black face and said, *Thanks, Mom, for all you haven't done today.*"

"*Ew.* Daddy, what's this?"

"Jesus Mary and—" Art snatched the Mills bomb from Lucy's hand, checked the pin, threw the thing as far as he could into the adjacent field, and then tackled his daughter to the ground.

"The pin's still in," he kept saying. "It was live, but the pin's still in." He said that for the rest of the day, and long into the night. Unexploded ordnance still comes up, in France, by the thousands of tons, each year.

61

HE WALKED

THEY WENT BACK in waves—one, two, three, four—bullets bursting their spines into splintering sprays. Each wave foundered, just like real ones do, before they do something dramatic (like swallow the earth, whole).

We can't stay here, Herald thought. Then a dog barked. Ostic, whose Lewis gun had remained with the forlorn hope to give covering fire, turned to see Jujitsu half wriggle her way out of Herald's leather jerkin. Bill was seeing stranger things, so returned to his rackety task, shouting at Fritz, between bursts, "MILLIONS NOW PRACTICE HAIR DRILL!"

Major Stock had tried to send her back before they reached the wire. Instead, she bounded through the gap, its white marker flag bloodied like an apron in an abattoir. There was gas pooling everywhere; it was only a matter of time before she went digging and filled her lungs with enough gas to drown a cow.

John Herald had already seen more death, and more animal death, than he cared to remember: Drowned puppies, drowned kittens on the farm where he grew up enough to run from and never talked about to anyone except Mary Helen, maybe. Maybe not even her. Too many dogs; too many cats. Drowned.

So when he saw the spindly form traversing the bridgework of crater lips that lifted clear of the gas pooling within, he took off his gloves, threw away his helmet, and flashed out of the Canadian lines like a level-headed thunderbolt.

The Germans, it must be said, did not target the dog—they used so many as messengers, and so few survived the bombardments and box barrages they were sent to get through. Did they spare John Herald, too, when they saw what he was after, the last man to come over from the Englanders' side that day?

The number of times a soldier, or entire bodies of men, did not fire, or did not fire to hit, will never be known. John was the last man over, and John with Jujitsu strapped to his chest was the last man back. Art and Bill would argue, in the years to come, whether or not, on that return journey, he had loped or just walked.

He walked.

62

NO FUCKING MONUMENT

THE MENIN GATE. Now, there's a thing for you. A gate that can't be closed, a block-long Arch of Absence, hollowed mausoleum for the hallowed unfound. Maybe it was those three enormous holes in the roof; maybe it was the rain drizzling through the central one onto his upturned face, but it's a little like building a temple over an outhouse because Jesus shat there, Bill thought, standing in the balance of the road, beneath those three Os, pawning their ellipsis to the sky.

Left out, left out to rot in No Man's Land, or simply anatomized by shellfire, nearly half a million of the Empire's million dead.

> HERE ARE RECORDED NAMES
> OF OFFICERS AND MEN WHO FELL
> IN YPRES SALIENT BUT TO WHOM
> THE FORTUNE OF WAR DENIED
> THE KNOWN AND HONOURED BURIAL
> GIVEN TO THEIR COMRADES
> IN DEATH

In Death on its own line. Bill liked that, the words capstoned above him as he strode into the gate from the city side. It was a directory of death. He squinted at them, not because he was trying to read them but because he could not take them in, at any level: 58,600 names in black on grey, titled by unit headings in gold. He squinted to keep them out, like sun, these black lights that went through the

Menin Road to the Salient, and then went out altogether. Names.

"William."

A woman, and there was only one who didn't call him Bill, or worse.

"Sister," he said, and touched his bright, blue beret with two yellowed fingers. The ash fell from the cigarette they held. Jenny was all smiles. He thought her the most fetching woman he had ever seen.

"William, Stan is … off with his memories. Will you walk me through it?" Bill didn't say, What memories could possibly be better than those with you, and you're actu-fucking-ally *here*, but the thought made him look down, stupidly.

"William," she repeated. Sweet Jack and Jesus, he thought; call an old soldier by his full name and he'll be puttees in your hands, unwrapped, undone, the circulation tingling up his calves.

"Is everything all right?" she asked. "Let's get out of the rain, at least."

Bill didn't move. Opened his mouth; shut it. Stole a glance at her, but she was giving hers away that moment.

"Sister, the truth of the matter is, I can't get any closer to those names than I am now."

Jenny put a hand on his arm. He mustn't look at her again.

"Say more," she said, really asking, just like a Bluebird should—neither prurient nor indifferent. Needing to know the exact dimensions of the wound, those cavities their bodies came wanting with. Cenotaphs.

"You see, coming on it here, first I thought, this is going to be some kind of … *fandango*: the Menin Gate! There was no fucking gate—begging your pardon, Sister—not even in the sense of an opening with no doors. And then I got to thinking like Stan: gate, gait. It was the *way* we walked through it, you know, the Vimy Glide. Only here, it wasn't the pace, it was the fact that you died going through it, and got this temporary pass to live on the other side. It wasn't a gate, it was a line. But that's not what bothers me."

She had taken his arm now, and they walked slowly towards what had been the Ypres Salient, that broad arrow of ordnanced earth, going grey in the drizzle and the dusk.

"It's those names, and no, it's not their number, or who they are, or did I know any of them — the Canadians have an entire arcade — it's that I can't focus on them and see the thing that holds them at the same time. And then these holes …"

"Wait a minute. What holds them, William?"

"Why …" and he looked a little startled at the question … *"death*, sister; death holds them, death with a capital *D.*"

"You're saying —"

"I'm saying, they really are here, they're not missing, but they should be. Death should have left them off the — no, it's life that — it's we the living who won't leave them be, out there. And then there are these holes."

They were beneath the outermost of these, walking while Bill talked, pausing when he had to think out loud. What a very different man you are, William Ostic, Jenny thought, from the blood-red demon Stan told me of. You, your face, the boundless grace of you. Underneath these glowing openings. They looked up. *What about the holes, William?* But she said nothing, waited for him to find the words he wanted. They didn't fit; it didn't matter. Men had come to her more broken than this, and all her magic was to let them go in. On, she meant on. The clouds actually broke in the west; slanting sun lit up the country like a green sea, and caught them against the glowing vast: man and woman, soldier and succor, standing in the gate.

"It's as much as to say, We made you come and go on the level, towards the horizon of death, or relief—you know what they say, Beyond the Horizon—and now, we've decided to let you come and go from heaven to earth, if you want."

Jenny game his arm a squeeze. "That's lovely, William."

"Is it, Sister?"

There were tears—something she had never seen—tears on his cheeks as he looked up, fixedly, trying to hide them in the rain. Something told her—no, she wasn't going to ask why.

"Why this bothers me is ... do you realize," he said, "realize, instead of know, just how many holes I put into people back then? I needed *permission* to do that. And now they've called the dead back to this funnel house and given them permission to remind us, the ones who killed, and lived, that we didn't die, too, but will, *and no fucking monument will cover that.*"

He was shaking in his trench coat; water dribbled off the shelf of his beret. She could almost hear his lungs shudder as he spat out his words like chaw. Our little hovel bodies, she thought.

"We were all willing, William," she said, almost mockingly, but with a smile, in that sonorous voice she reserved for special patients.

"Yeah? ... Well ... Come on, Sister; let's get us a drink."

Jenny grabbed his arm again, practically wrung it from him and tucked it under her left breast. Cenotaphs, gates, wounds, holes, halls of absence. She wanted to fill something, if not fulfill it.

"No, brother William; let's get us a *room.*" And they swung back towards the Grande Place.

63

ON THE BRIDGE

THE PIGS were on the bridge, that much he could see. The
Bathurst Street Bridge, herding south, like a choppy, dirty-
pink sea. How they got there, who drove them, or led them,
was harder to tell. They were on the bridge, squealing like
a hundred streetcars sliding to a stop, and failing, in the
dull, early dawn of a wet, winter morning in Toronto. Which
meant the ground was white-brown mud with soot frosting.
Galloping was out of the question. Horseshoed hooves
thucked up and plunged, into damp snow, over wet ice, slid
on silver rails and almost shivered their forelegs to pieces
as they rose and fell—and Constable Jim Wardle did, too,
his remount (he always thought of the horses as remounts,
since the originals had been donated to the army overseas),
Dandy, cascading into a snowbank, which broke its fall and
saved Jim's leg from breaking with it.

There were now figures among the swine—two he could
see, clearly—rising and falling as they, too, slipped and fell,
one red, one green, without hats on their heads and, my
God, they were girls. And the animals were all shapes and
sizes, racing over the railway corridor as if possessed.

Jim knew there was something biblical about that, which
flashed inanely through his mind at the same time he
wondered why the pigs were being driven to slaughter in
such a bizarre way. He could see the Park-Blackwell abattoir
clear as thinking, looming out of the haze on the far side of
the bridge, almost adjacent to the old blockhouse from the
fort. It was a foggy morning; it had rained overnight in the

midst of a snap, and the pigs ran on like the heralds of a dim new dawn.

Sap could hardly see for the blood on her face had begun to congeal in the cold. She had been struck on the head with the back of a meat hook and half her auburn hair was matted red — as if she were wearing a busby, Jim thought, his horse among the pigs now, which only drove them faster than before. Her body woozed and yawed, and her arms were stretched for balance, but she fell, fell, and then, got up again.

She was amid the trusses of the bridge when steam blasted either side of her upward as a train thundered under; the officer was enveloped in it, and Sapphira turned to see him ride clear through — nightmare, she thought. Alley, she thought. She instinctively reached in her pocket and brought up — marbles! A fistful of puries she had won at school — okay, well, stolen — and heaved them at the horse's feet, which had no effect other than to soften Jim's already beaten heart — it was such a useless gesture.

64

OTHER GODS

No one disappears in open prairie, and yet, there is
no other place on earth as lonely as these flat fields, made
flatter still by the plough and whisked clean by the dust
bowl into an aerodrome for the moon. Visions. It sometimes
amazed him there weren't more of them than there already
were: a boy, working solitary in a wheat field—with horses
no less—Fred had seen shapes making for him from miles
away. Masks, mostly, with hooked noses and badly painted
features, careless, slap-dash. He'd turn from the stook he'd
just righted and there it would be, leering, jeering, and then
go knock down another one.

Stooks were one thing; people were something else. How
many arms and hands had fed themselves into the thresher
that way? Something bumped them. And only Fred would
see—the boy Fred, the Fred who had yet to hear the call,
the voice crying in the void that did for wilderness out there.
Of course, wheat fields are simply rotten with resurrection,
so it came as no surprise to see Him coming, swinging a
flaming sword, twirling it like a drum-major's baton at the
end of the row.

"There are other gods," he said, "but they cannot resist me."

And Fred was just old enough, and still young enough, to
ask, "Why not?"

"Because my truth makes a highway of the mountains," he
said. "Because my truth makes it all come out in the wash.
Heaven is here, a place of exposure pure, where the spirits of
the dead wave like sheaves. You can skim your hand along

the tops of them, and each tingle communicates a life. That's why it isn't boring, up there."

Fred smirked his little-boy smirk, the one he used to cover his failings at school.

"Believe in me, and the masks will go away. Believe in me, and you will never see them again."

But will they be gone? Fred didn't ask that, and the Son of Man is a sly one. So he took the boy on strength, and mighty hallelujahs rang out over the barbed wire fences. And so he rattled along the Prairie roads, squaring the O of earth with the same, fatal certainty.

She must be found. No one disappears out here, in this resistless, relentless emptiness.

65

HOLD ME JUST

THEY DID NOT GET FAR. Jenny and Bill turned to find
the Menin Gate filling up with a crush of veterans—ex-
Imperials, Bill (correctly) guessed—waiting for the
honour guard that, each dusk, plays the *Last Post* within
the monument. Bill let his arm slip from Jenny's but, as the
crowd hemmed them up against the marble wainscotting,
they held hands almost without intention. The trumpets are
silver and terrifically clear, played by Belgian firemen who are
used to their effect within that sound-box of stone.

But neither Bill nor Jenny had heard anything like it.
Sword and buckler, pierce and echo, boom and recoil, all
at once. Bill saw searchlights flashing from the decks of
channel destroyers protecting troopships at night; Jenny, the
horizon on fire with the bombardment that preceded the
battle of Amiens. And someone, somewhere, she thought
to herself, had brought a hound that bayed within this …
funhouse of loss. She stopped, struck by the coinage while
the voice, inhuman, of the veritable beast that had mawed
them all, sharded with wimpers and rent with howls, sent
shivers up and down their spines.

They drew closer. Bill put one arm on her shoulder
and the other on her waist and it was, curiously, by these
gestures that both knew no room would be forthcoming
or necessary. It's not that they were humbled out of sex or,
worse, spooked from adultery by the mewling of the dog; a
simple regard for each other's well-being seized them both,
differently; Jenny feeling how unfair it would be to Bill to

have to maneuver and dissemble in front of his friend, and Bill, that she was something the war preserved, for once, something good it brought back — why tear into that with blunted desire, virility long spent, mechanized? Proficiency and mass murder had joined up early to wean him off sex for life.

So he thought. So did she. It was past dusk when she pushed him back up the stairs to the wings, turned him around — kaleidoscoped with names — with her wordless mouth, and led him into the small Commonwealth War Grave that runs along the old stone-faced earthworks that once starred Ypres entire. There was that fucking moat, Bill thought; and she wondered for the camera that caught her in his eye if the swans who dipped and sailed in there were the same as those who — and down they went, in the dark, among the white teeth of earth-sown soldiers. It was quick work; they were hardly undressed. And meant more and less than love or even war can ever grasp.

How does he keep his hands off you? But he didn't ask. Just reached for what he could beneath her woolens and the past. He wept like a drunkard not during but after, and couldn't keep the gasper in his mouth. And she was surprised at his hands — machinist hands, admittedly quick and nimble, that actually knew where and how and when to reduce her to putty. Puttees, she laughed to herself (for she and he hardly exchanged a word up there, more from the needlessness of it, given Bill's — and here she laughed right out loud — skill in handling her) — and that is what gave the game away: he was a Lewis-gunner, dammit, trained to strip, oil, and reassemble more moving parts than anyone would guess quite literally blindfolded. What was dusk or middle age for that matter to his sure, precise manner?

Bill had never been with a free woman before.

✳

"What keeps you alive, out there?"

"The hope of fucking you one more time."

"What keeps you here?"

"The hope of fucking you one more time."

"Anything else?"

"The hope of fucking you one more time."

"And when you go up the line, do you ever stop hoping?"

"We never stop hopping, Sister; we hop from hope to napoo pretty quickly."

"You mean as in, just now?"

Bill laughed his staccato laugh—a rarity. You didn't know he had a girl. Well, he didn't. But sometimes he got close enough to slip sidewise through the back door of an estaminet and find himself an *avec*.

The rattle of his hands on her breasts—the Belgian Rattlesnake, he told her (nickname for the Lewis gun, for the sound it made, but); in truth, he could not hold his hands still anymore. And so he always thought of squeezing off individual rounds, or two together, when his fingers dug lightly into the flesh there he so wanted to touch. And each time his unsteady hands held her there, trembling inward like two pulsing jellyfish in a sea of soft, the invisible butt of his Lewis gun would kick back against his shoulder, like a solid, ghost limb, so that he actually shook back every time he took hold of her. One round. Two.

He was not a violent or even aggressive lover—if you take that from the above, I have failed altogether in my object. War makes all things violent through you—all things shook Bill; for him, violence to himself was the through-well of experience. He did not pass it on.

"The *fuck* stops here," he said to himself, thinking of that.

"I do not think so, Mister Canada" (she spoke English well; was the second of four daughters, in a small house with a pale ball lit in the window: *Moon for Sale*), "I don't think it ever, ever does."

"Oh I didn't mean you, miss," Bill said, as his pay went into her bright hands.

"You mean, you want to be kind. Kill and be kind, is that it?"

"Kill and be damned for it, but not you, miss—"

"*Sabrevois*. It means to see with the sword of war. My father was in *Soixante-douze*; I was born when he was on campaign against the Prussians. At Metz, we learned, he died a hero's death, and then came a note from his pocket, blood-stained as all such notes are *de rigeur*, telling maman to call me Sabrevois, for the briefness of life, and the sight of war that took it from him."

Bill is all attention.

"We go again?" she said, evenly.

Yes, he says. And takes his time. Yes, she says, and takes him in.

"Stan sent me to find you."

Jenny nodded. She owed him for that, she thought, and wondered, would he even care? And on what basis? Two men on a match, she thought, watching Bill's fingers shake with the matchsticks he could barely light. She wanted to tuck them back inside her like shirttails, and then she remembered where they were—Ypres, the Cloth Hall, fabric centre of the world beyond the sea.

"Hold me just a little, William," she answered.

66

LOIS SLEPT

AN EXTRA RAP at Lois's front door, so sharp it makes the sisters jump. No bell for this latecomer. If that's what it is. An extra? Jenny asked Lo between the lines of her forehead. *Rapety-rap-rap*. A cane? A walking stick with a sword in it?

"I'll just see who that is," Lo said, disingenuously.

"I'll go with you," Jenny added, still on guard but losing ground. Fast.

The sisters said nothing, but you could feel the room relax a little, ease back into its darkened corners. It was late. They heard Lois work the locks, and Jenny said ... then nothing. There was no sound at all. Then, footsteps in the hall, one set up the stairs, two others into the parlour. Loud whispering. Grace guessed who it was, but said nothing, before Major Margaret Macdonald, humble as a janitor, swept into the room, to see this world's supply, its own superlative foundation, reduced to these few, a mere handful.

We are so munitioned, Jenny thought — some of us, anyway — we are so larded with the sublime, when young, if the world turns our way. It doesn't for all of us. It didn't for Lo. No world for her ecstasy. But it did for her — for Margaret Macdonald, impossibly, now, here; and for Jennabeth Gray, who saw her come through the door of the tent in the Casualty Clearing Station like the first female rough-rider, to check up on her girls, in person, in France. That was the one near Val-des-soucies, where she first saw Adelaide, busting her gut to keep a tourniquet in twist. Here, let me help you, Jenny had said, and Lo had let fly.

Jenny didn't really hear the words. All she saw, that first day in, near the Front, within shouting distance of the guns (gun-shouts, it must be said, extend much farther than ours; Casualty Clearing Stations were as close to the Front as nursing sisters were allowed, provided that that same affront to all they represented didn't fly right over them, or come up under them, dropping and swirling their wordless away)—I say, all that she saw was how wounded she was—Adelaide. Not the boy without a leg to stand on, nor even the vast tide of wounded rising from the *sappage* of Amiens, that great victory. Truly, it was. But Jenny saw nothing else, really, for days after. The wounded she had seen before. They were terrible, indescribable—over the top. You had to shut them out in order to help them in any way.

But this woman, with the fluted fingers and the blonde, wan, tapestry face; this pale dame who should have been somewhere else—and on a palfrey, worked in scarlet and gold: she'd never seen anything like it before. Such ... longing. Of course it was the war. But more, something less than she suspected and more than she could conceive, so that the first time the two of them shared an afternoon away from carnage they simply drove their borrowed bicycles to the nearest *petit chambre* they could find.

Lo closed the door, turned and then Jenny—not her, not Elizabeth, not at first—tore into her clothing like fresh earth over an infanticide. She couldn't bear it. It wasn't what she touched, or even how transcendently Lois came actually over her. It was something behind that ribcage, beneath her knee-caps, stuck in her skull. A screaming, driving, starving need. Sex was just the way to feed it. Jenny was crazy with what Lo wanted—they weren't giving each other anything as they fumbled with familiar garments and strange ecstasy.

That scar, that never-healing wound, wound into Lo's side like seams of tar, healed them, when, after an hour or more of more contact than either of them had ever felt possible, Lois slept in her arms and she slept.

You mean to say this was going on? I mean to say that war was ongoing; certain stories can't be told. For the nursing sisters that Canada sent overseas, this was multiply true: to think that Major Macdonald could care for her charges as intimately as she did, even from her office in London, and not know which ones were sleeping together would be as absurd as her not knowing who was engaged to which winning officer. She enthused over and supported marriage—she knew so few would get, or want, the chance when they got home. It wasn't sex and it wasn't independence so much as untranslatability: thrilled to be in the war, thrilled to be near the Front, thrilled to be with each other. Thrilled by the killing, too? No, but you can see how easily the one could be mistaken for the other. So they said nothing.

Which is precisely what Lois said when she woke, puffy with a nap that had lasted, in her mind, for decades. Are *you* here? Then they made love right proper, giving instructions, asking for how and for what and for when. They were sisters; bodies didn't faze them at all.

Nothing. Said nothing. They never said, during the course of the war, a single, solitary word to each other, outside of those rooms, that dripped with love.

But it was an unusual November and Macdonald was dripping. She shook her scarlet armour off—her cloak, that is—her bluebird's cowl, lined with war. Jenny took both cloak and hat upstairs. Lo took Margaret into the parlour.

"You've *got* to convince her."

"My dear, she's a grown—"

"Woman, don't tell me. I've noticed long enough. And I've waiting for fucking ever. Use your authority."

"In matters of the heart my dear … all right," Margaret said, changing course ever so slightly, heading for a different port altogether.

"Jennabeth," she called when she heard her footsteps coming back down the main stairs. "A word with you." Couple it with something, Lo cracked; but she kept her mouth shut. This was serious.

"Are you still married to Athelstan Allward?"

"In mind and body, yes; if spirits count for nothing, we're hitched to the moon."

Lo snorted. *Shut up*.

"You know, I once had a patient, in Panama, who starved himself to death. Every day I'd part the mosquito netting and there would be less of him. On his bedside table was a pile of letters. I asked him, one day, if he would like me to re-read them to him. *Dear Silas*, they began. *Dear Silas*, and always ended, *Your ever-loving, Anne*. Until one day a card came announcing the marriage of one Anne Carmichael to whoever it was had actually acted on all that desire. I didn't even try to feed him after that. I knew he wanted to be dead. Now, that's settled," she concluded, almost forgetting her audience. "Pray, show me in."

67

CLEAR *THAT*

SHE WOKE UP by the roadside with her head in his lap and leaves in the sky. An elm tree umbrella'd above them. He looked down at her, the sky in his eyes. How could that be? The sky was behind him, above them both, screened by leaves but there and arctic blue. How could it be both there and in his eyes, as he looked down at her, stroked a cheek, his other hand on her ribs as if he were about to strum them, loose but live, lithe, wise to the sound-box of her sighs?

And where had they been, all the night last and into the dawn? Blaze nickered nearby, untied, grazing by the margin of the road, a sleek knot of crepuscular muscle, moulded into horse. She remembered the train (there were no night trains on that particular line, but that seemed to matter less than what had followed): the not-landing, her mind falling instead into blind wonder at the soaring dark, which thickened into cloud (she had thought, crazily, that they had landed on the engine and that it was steam), which gave way to ground, ground she had never seen and from a height no one ... there were what she first took for little ponds, and shelter belts rust red, and cracks in the earth that came closer and closer.

She saw a mass of men loping along under hats that shone dull — like turtle shells — above their dun; saw a crawling rectangle tractioned round with belts of whirr; and then one man running, then two, then three and the third was John and *whump*! Blaze hit the ground galloping; John's strength no longer backed her — he ran, behind the horse now, to catch her, hatless, heedless, that lightning stride she once saw in the fields, gathering grain against the storm. She grabbed the blazing mane and rode flat out — arms grasping, legs clasping — until she saw the hedge and knew, Clear *that* and there'd be no coming back, she'd be with him forever, never have to leave him, trees in his eyes, sky winking down at her, tuck hooves rampant, leap over, rump under, buck and *SNAP!*

She fell back into barbed wire; they'd never cleared the ground.

She woke up by the roadside with her head in his lap and with leaves in his eyes. "Oh, Johnny. Did you land in *that*?" A belt of wire overgrown with shelter. "Is *that* what happened?"

"I was going to die anyway," he said, without a trace of regret. "She made sure I could come back." Mary Helen thinks he's talking about the horse.

"Why did you wait so long?"

"It wasn't my decision."

"That's not the John Herald I know."

"It wasn't my decision."

"Whose, then? The horse's? Who decided, Johnny?"

"It concerns time, and the span of our lives, and what we need, and when we need it. It was my decision to come back, but it was yours, really — well, kind of — it was kind of your decision, by the way you were living, I mean."

"That's clear as mud."

"You think there's an explanation for everything."

"Sometimes."

"But there's a difference between what you call an explanation, and what I call a reason. And what I call a reason isn't a cause. I call it a reason because it's something we do in our minds."

"What—what do we do, John?"

"We don't do anything, out here," (he was strumming her now, her heart thrumming under ginger gingham) "it's something we do *in*, not out, like how the future steps out of you."

"I can't believe I'm talking to you this way. You never used to talk like this."

"Sure I did. I just talked about different things. Objects, mainly. Driving fence posts. Tending animals."

And you know something, Mary Helen thought to herself, he was right. His mind switched from side to side, horse-tail swift, swatting away any attempt to get a fix on him, sting him into substance. He had always been like this.

"Tell me something about you I don't know," John said then. "Tell me something I missed by coming back so late."

"Just my life, Johnny. The life I never had with you. It's funny, but I can feel it now, like a ghost limb, I can actually extend my foot and put it on, like a new boot that you somehow always wore but never wore down. I can feel your return—the real one, the one that never happened. The days driving those fence posts together—me holding one up, you resting on your maul, squinting at the camera. I'm all smiles, of course. My beautiful boy, back from the war, the wilderness, back at last. Back even from himself"—and she gave a hard look into those sky eyes crossed with clouds. "I can even feel the children we didn't have—two, a boy and a girl—the girl's the eldest—and—"

But there was no *and*. Just a car door slamming, and the voice of Fred Abercrombie, powerful, urgent, relieved:

"We've been looking all over for you."

68

OUT OF GRACE

HE WANTED IT, like most things, to be over. To find some
quiet corner by himself where he could savour, singly, what
had happened to so many. His own world. In this case, at the
ceremony, at Vimy, there was no world left to savour. The
battlefield "finds" were merely junk that no one had yet had
the time to throw away. The archaeology of the Western
Front frightened him more than had the living un-animal,
its sudden guns rust red, their unending thrum folded at
last beneath the soil. Untold dugouts and tunnels and caves
bubbled under terra none too firma. So much determined
cheerfulness! Their bodies blasted beyond recovery, less
able than the dead to cover themselves in forgetfulness, like
that figure of Canada, athletic brooder, hooded mother with
the sinews of Achilles.

Is that why Allward's statues were so virile? You needed a
lot of energy to remember; the living were not up to it, and
their children were as far removed from it as a fairy-tale.
Which is as it should be, Stan thought. Walter Allward, no
relation, was a diminutive man, but had dreamt the dead
aided the living in the time of battle. Stan believed this; he
also believed the dead wanted nothing to do with Returned
Men — they had little enough time left: let them have a shot
at something like living.

That's what Stan saw, anyway, when the King pulled
the cord and the Ensign fell from Canada, personified.
She stood on the massive base like a lone passenger on a
stone ship, tossing towards the pyramidal slag-heaps of

Lens. Maternal patriarch (*a mother of a father*, was how Bill put it), head bent, sheaf in hand, with eyes that—when you got under them, it was like looking into a wind cloud—hollowed out the livid air.

The unveiling had shocked him, and not just for its simplicity, or that barrelling stare. He'd seen Allward's work before; he knew about allegory—a strange medievalism haunted these very modern bodies. But this one told him something straightaway that years of suffering and reflecting had never made clear:

For we had at last waged Christian war, Stan reasoned to himself, fought the first truly Christ-like ... you see—it's not just that in death there is no victory; it's that death is the victory. The soldiers were not warriors—that was for Troy and Carthage—they were sacrifices. On the altar of technology that ground their bones to a halt at the foot of the cross each one was made to bear: shovels and picks, yes, but the whole progression of it, the West, whatever that meant, to the Western Front, from the beginning of time till now. War had been winnable. This one wasn't—but we fought on anyway, and how we fought! Without hope. Without faith. And grace, my God, my God, did not take up the slack.

Ours, Stan concluded, is a nation born out of grace. As in out of wedlock. Married to a deadlock of nations overseas. And now, the generation underground seemed to lift their mouths through the sagging soil and gave a great cry: we died in such a place, which neither hope nor mercy graced. It was elementary; it was obvious. It hit him right between the eyes. Calvary, technology; this graceless face.

So he reasoned, as he wandered over broken ground, grown grassy but not flat, just a little on his own, his boot soles sounding dimly in the caverns underfoot.

69

SEMI-COLON

HER ICE BOAT FLOATS into the bay, its passengers are
two: Sapphira and her castaway, Flavella, almost blue with
cold. Jim has already hauled his horse around and heads
for the nearest call box; Sap can hear Alley's voice and
Jim's blending like a high violin and a kettle drum, the one
stretched to scraw the skies, the other pounding down to
keep her from splitting her strings. Sap is numb; her head
has stopped flowing and Flavella is half inside her frozen
coat. The bay has broken open and the ice falls into the
current rushing through the Western Gap.

She'd hugged the horse and wept into its neck before
Flavella hit the ice floe, and she tore herself away from the
constable's charger and yelled as if her bloodied garments
were one big tongue and the horse made out of metal. She
fell in once — that soaked her good — and would have gone
under but for the piles of the old wharf still studding the
surface, deadheads from a city that had sunk beneath the
bay. Flavella reached a chunk of ice no bigger than a parlour
room and scrabbled from edge to edge, the floating, flat
world of her Ptolemaic mind at last concluding enough
was enough. She tipped into Sapphira as the latter leapt on
board, tackling the animal as she did so and falling into a
comma, curled around a period of pig.

Semi-colon, semi-coma, semi-conscious twain. They
heard voices on the shore. They saw a line of trees. Walking,
Sap believed, walking over water to where — and then she
passed out, the cold cupping her body, a hand on fire.

70

FUCKING NOTHING

STAN GOT UNSTEADILY to his feet—Christ, how
conventional is that, he thought, and Art, as he steadied him,
would have replied, Don't underestimate convention, Mate.
It's how we get most things done. Stan certainly was, with
more Belgian beer spilling out of him than an open barrel
pulled along a cobblestone road. He waved Art away and for
once, with Lucy and her mother to look after elsewhere, Art
let his lieutenant have his way.

Something was missing, and it wasn't just his wife, or
the mate he'd sent after her (and why is that, I wonder?
Why didn't Stan go himself? Why send Bill?). The most
ubiquitous, least noticeable, and above all, particular
factor—Stan was unhappy with the word: it had too much
of the delusion of control about it—and *particular* was good,
in the sense of particles, but *peculiar* would be our term, so
far, at any rate. Gas. It was ... everywhere you turned in the
mid to late stages of the war. Mustard gas, the gas that lasted,
lay in wait. It was the one horror no one wanted even to have
to avoid talking about, like desertion. It was a shame—pale
words!—to whomever used it. Victory by gas meant that
the earth and all that was in or on or about it were doomed
indeed. It meant victory by omnicide.

He wandered up to the restored walls fronting the moat
by the Menin Gate. How few statues boasted of that! Victory
by gas. What would a statue to that be, but plinth, alone?
Possibly with a lingering vee somehow hanging in the air
above it, like fire-light on cigarette smoke, or moonlight

on fog, accompanied by the vaguely audible sound of thousands upon thousands of men, coughing, gasping, and retching their insides quite literally, out.

The smell of urine was everywhere; at the Front, it had serious competition. But at these veterans' gatherings, you had two things that ensured olfactory supremacy: an abundance of drink, and men who had the right to piss where they damned well pleased. Here in the cemetery it was particularly strong. Tears. Territory. Bill and Jenny making a composite divining rod at the end of the stone row.

He was never sure what he saw, he turned away so quickly. Unseen. He fervently prayed. Never sure what surprised him most: the quick prayer he said for both of them — or the fact that he had expected to find them here. He knew it. He had, after all, sent him. He wasn't god-for-fucking *Croix de guerre* for fucking nothing.

71

THE EX-VETS

IT'S HARD FOR US TO CONCEIVE of just how happy a
Depression-era band could be. A jazz, not a big, band, with
cornet, banjo, and trumpet; bass, tenor, and clarinet; sax,
tempo, and drum set. The instruments glowed dully in the
lanterns hung from hand-forged hooks or looped under
beams — there was some nonsense about having to muck
out a space for the drums in swine-time.

By happy, I mean the sound they made out of those
essentially old-world instruments, a sound that came from
before the war and sprung from a sorrow and suffering
as great — if such things can be measured — and of far
greater duration than Great War itself. To come upon a
jazz ensemble in the 1930s; to hear that very sound in an
estaminet back of the Front in the 1910s — as these men had,
all of them former soldiers — had once been as common as it
would seem unlikely, to us.

They were city men, called themselves *The Ex-Vets*, and
made the trip out to Roland from Winnipeg, more often
than not, in the back of farmer's trucks sent to fetch them,
or fetch them in, as Fred liked to say, making their tympanic
majesties part and parcel (or, to swing it, smart and partial)
to and with the harvest, that medley of maturity taken in,
the foison of acreage in the spring of their steps. *Winter Will
Come* — an old favourite — bumped and squeaked amid the
shuffling of cattle and the occasional neigh, for they were
here — the Abercrombies and Pritchards, the Loblaws, the
Watsons — and all of their neighbours, mounting the mow

for the one, big blowout the season allowed. Dancers above; band below — glad animal movements, Stan would have quoted, had he been there.

That's what John was thinking, suddenly missing his friend and his concert-parting ways. He wasn't there, of course, but she was — and at his urging. Her arm lingered among the feeding troughs and chased a hay from her absent-minded hair as Fred watched her, astonished. That she should be here! She took her place awkwardly, with the sort of broken grace that new-walking children have, who bend the rhythm of whatever they are doing to suit their own make-believe. And she, Mary Helen, could only make believe he was here, who once held her, her heralder, her Johnny Long Gone.

"Devil May Care," someone called out — one of Elgin Pritchard's hired men — and *The Ex-Vets* swung into full mood. They were like a floating island of speaking trumpets, a blaring tumbleweed of hope amid the rolling O's of dust-bowl yields, the new sound that the old ground had concealed, lain in against the winter of the world. And Fred swung her, all right, he deftly turned her without insisting, and she followed, only half-resisting the desire to finally give up the ghost. Did John watch, up there in the hay loft? Did he toss his straw locks down, cast off at last?

Not bloody likely. The only ghost she was looking to give up was her own. She loved the actual sweat Fred left on the inside of her forearm when they crossed each other in the choreography of the great, too late, insatiate. Henceforward, all bodies would be like these, swung out among the stars, stabled with human kine, with what passed for kindness revealed as pure joy.

72

HELLO, GOODBYE

STAN SAT ON THE EDGE of the seat of Mons, and said, nothing. He sat on the edge of the seat of war. The end and the beginning, the Canadians and the Germans — old comrades, now. Her infidelity. Was his fidelity. That's what she — said to him, when he confessed to finding the two of them — oiled like disassembled Lewis guns: twin mounted, drying lightly — in the Commonwealth War Graves plot plopped right on top of Vauban's original, geophysical plan for the town. Geometrical did not seem the right word anymore. Europe's greatest master of polygonal dirt, the genius that dropped star fortifications on tactile (tactical didn't seem the right word here, either) earth from the fool's paradise of an impregnable haven — the pre-reason dream that someone could be counted on never to give way.

His fidelity meant starve the warm garrison within her, those blue-cloaked, scarlet-lined *comeradoes*, doe-eyed and hearts afire — was that what she meant? She didn't see her body like that. Her infidelity, the — don't say *brute* — fact of it struck him like a clod of mud. Passing lorry. Sorry. Passing sorrow.

No matter you could see it coming like a mule train in phosphor on a moonless night in June. It's that there were no fenders on her chastity. Charity? Something of that order seemed implied (he knew next to nothing about Lo, not to mention Sap and Alley, to which he could hear his former sister ask, What about you and me, to her, or you and John, to the both of us, differently?).

Not to mention you and your whole fucking platoon, Art added, practically, vis-à-vis everybody else. And, laying out beyond that, outwork after outwork of covered ways for his heart to beat in supported autonomy: the concert party, D Company, the entire battalion, the Canadian Corps, the living or the dead. But her body, as he knew it — *The Great Awe as I Saw It*, he joked, sardonically — who had taken that from him? John and Blaze and somehow his kid sister, showing up in the re-recaptured ex-British now-German trench system, running from traverse to traverse, until he finally lost the weight of it.

"Is the horse, you? Are you the horse, too?" he had wailed. And who should be with him in that maze of amazement, deracinated like an under-dug tree, its roots tugging at the passing webbing? Stan lost his train of thoughts. No, it was Bill Ostic who'd been with him then, and got them out, storming their own side by mistake, charaded in German rain capes, under cover.

Nothing hidden about Vauban — at least at Ypres. That moat, those stones, these swans. Art's best mate, and the fighter — not the soldier (that was Art) nor yet the warrior (that was John) — the *fighter* he most admired, then and now. If only because he knew of his (lack of) manner with women.

No, she had broken from him, who had broken through to him. Saying she had broken for him, who was broken now. He sat on the sharp edge of alpha, his heels on pillowed omega, and wept. For Mons. For Mons. *Pubis. Veneris.* Mons.

This was their last, first, second stop: Mons, the last battle in the war. Stan was gone, by the time the Canadians got there; invalided home, Not Yet Diagnosed (Nervous). Gone and buried — his hair in her apron, her hand on his thigh, his heart in her eyes, saying, goodbye. Hello. Goodbye.

73

MAKE ME HAPPY

THEY MADE LOVE in the usual way, breasts and hips and thighs;
they made love and said nothing. One set of sighs. Hers.

"Johnny?"

"Mmph."

"You don't feel right, do you?"

"What do you mean?"

"Feel," she said, and put his hand to her breast. "You don't
feel like you used to, do you?"

"You're as fine as the first time I laid a hand on you."

She gave the required half-smile. It was too dark to see it,
but she had learned that John saw everything. "That's not
what I mean."

"I'm not shell-shocked. That never meant anything to me."

She paused. Hot wet turning cold. He could tell she—and
she, well, she just had to know, sooner or later.

"I mean you can't feel me, really, can you? I can feel you,
but you can't, me, is that right?"

John said nothing. Then, before she could come to
conclusions, "It's not nothing. That I feel. Nothing."

"What is it, then? What am I to you, now, Johnny?" And
she put his hand here and there as she said again, like the
school teacher she was, "What," breast, "am," neck, "I," thigh,
"to," belly, "you" and left him there, between her legs that
shivered a little with the cold. Hand or her? Prairie, chilled.
Autumn coming down and nothing done, the yard unswept,
the grass uncut, the house unkempt from porch to eaves.

"Johnny? You don't really, I don't make you hap—"

"Goddamn it, Emaiche!" He'd withdrawn his hand.

"I guess I'm what you'd call thin on the ground." A long pause. "It's not as if there's a curtain or something between us. Where you feel rain, I feel mist. Where you feel sun, I feel moonlight. Nobody can make me happy. That's not why I'm here."

She couldn't see him at all. It was pitch black in the room and his voice bounced lightly off the walls, like a bat caught indoors. He seemed to be everywhere and nowhere at once, sonar in place of contact.

"And why might that be, Johnny dear?" She paused, then answered for him: "To make me say goodbye to you. To be the one, who dies, to you."

"Now, where did you pick that up? That's not you. You know full well this makes it worse. You came anyway. You can't make someone uniquely happy, John, unless they're a child, which I'm not, or unless they're reconciled to solitude, which I kind of am, and never will be. I will always want you, in me."

A pause, and then a thrill of fear through her joints, a spike of ice-water, freshet of glacial spring: *he was gone.* Was he, gone? And she held herself suspended in the terror and relief of it, just as she had when he first appeared — *only backwards*, she said to herself, in that genuinely childlike way she still had.

And then John was beside her in the bed again. "We've done other things," he said.

"That ride," she said.

"That train," he said.

"That sky," she said.

"Again," he said.

"Don't die," she said.

194

74

SING US HOME

What pairings survived that catastrophe?
What lines came out even, what lines at all?
There were only two, and they did not rhyme:
even that coupling broke down, eventually.
We, who survived, who stand apart, alone
with our memories, though we seem to form a block
of faces typecast with the dexterity
of honour, what is it we have left
to be thankful for? Peace. Peace? We cannot hear
lyre or sonnet. Our lives live, buried
over there. What muse can muster them?
What inspired bard, ordinary Orpheus,
casualty report, battalion diary,
lost letters home, paybook stamped deceased,
what gathering around the hole of no
can sing the slightest part of what we know?

STAN PAUSED, put the pages down. He had begun with
Leading's overture, which, in this reconstructed Ypres of
1936, was like putting ham with eggs. The men loved it,
their wives bore it, and the bartenders reaped the benefit
of a brasserie-turned-estaminet full to bursting with happy
Canadians. The irreality of it all was overwhelming. This
was not *Partout*, some fakery staged inside the coliseum
of their lionized past; the Belgians had rebuilt the entire
town, with real stone, mortar, and brick: glazed clay and
stained glass, and those set-back gable ends that looked

like communication trenches run up to and from the sky.
Stan kept waiting for the first shell to fall. And now, he was
waiting for applause.

> Tell me the truth about what happened, there.
> The thing is, even if someone were to ask
> that of any one of us, neither song nor sacrilege,
> nor even simple, plain speaking would do
> duty for what our youths stood over.
> The most eloquent battalion histories
> are lists: names, dates, wounds, addresses.
> And yet we want to hear, the heart confesses
> a need for something like a shape
> to put it in, an urn for ashes
> past recalling to their shattered bones.
> It's not that I think I'm capable
> of doing whatever the hell passes
> for truth, but will try to sing us home.

He can feel Jenny smile at the incipient sonnet poking
its head up through the last 14 lines, shaking the locks of its
disheveled sestet like a child buried in leaves. The men shift
uncomfortably, worried that their wives won't like it, but the
women relax into the smoke. For once, someone is coming
within a million miles of what they have to deal with on a
daily basis.

Stan sees her, and sees, too, for the first time this trip, that
she is proud of him, still shines for him — those eyes. She
doesn't wear glasses for distances, and has even removed her
shades in the sunlight that slants over the Grande Place like
stage lighting. And he wants her, right now, on the bottled-
up tables, rolling on the tear-stained floor.

75

GAVE WAY

THE GROUND GAVE way beneath his feet. At first, he thought—even as he fell, he thought—this must mean I'm in a dream. So that when he woke, at the bottom of the hole, why, then waking had seemed waking indeed. He woke, but to the dream's reality, which was as unreal as he was unhurt. He woke on his back, but not from his rest; he woke on his back with a knife through his chest. A bayonet, fresh with wet rust, thrust itself through his ... tunic? He could tell by the runnel that he felt in the dark, running up on either side like bastard pointing.

This was war. Had peace been a dream? How had he come again to be in khaki? And then, he could hear Jenny shouting down, which only made him more confused. Was she trying to wake him? Was he really asleep? And if so, when he woke, would he still be wounded, as he was now, with the business end of a Lee Enfield making a dummy of his chest? He felt no pain, just a freshening sense of loss, of spillage; his heart leapt to the task of pumping him out, as if he were bailing the boat of his body, flush with blood.

He didn't speak. He was spoken to.

"Sssstan. Sssstan." A spark, and someone lit a brazier near the centre of the room. It was a dugout, he could see, instantly, thick with the fug of guttering candles stuck into shell casings hung from the walls. Dirt walls. Dry mouths.

"Sssstan."

There were soldiers. They shuffled in from the very earth, crumbled free from the corners and came forward, gas-masked, gloved, not an inch of flesh showing. And Stan felt like he did when he went to see the Two-Headed Man at the Exhibition before the war: cheated.

"Ladies and gentlemen, the Two-Headed Man really did exist, but he didn't live very long. This is what he would have looked like, had he lived." And a goon with a prosthetic head on his shoulder walked out from behind a painted screen of canvas.

"For crying in the beer," his mother had said. "Good night," she had added, getting up in high dudgeon.

But Stan could not.

76

SAP PNEUMATICA

She wakes on the ice in Toronto bay; wakes to a world of waking dreams, to the same old world, given a three-quarter turn. Spirits will never ask you for the time; they are always now. And Sapphira's pneumatic present inflates itself inside the body of a horse, some eight months hence, running riderless beneath a skyshell coped with clangour and bang.

We can be very specific, here: it is 8th August, 1918, the Black Day of Ludendorff's stormy legions, halted, like the Romans before (and against) them, by a single, liquid syllable: Marne, Rhine — river borders that speak volumes of fire. Gorged on victory, they cannot cross the Marne. It is the first day of the Amiens offensive, the beginning of almost unbridled Allied victories. This one is slamdunked by the twin dominions: Australia and Canada, supported by tanks and — wonders — cavalry, which comes into its own in the open fields that wave up beneath their advance.

The horse belongs to the Fort Garry Horse, part of the Canadian Cavalry Brigade. It is what you call a grey — as white as horses get on the Western Front — and it has been up against machine guns and down under drumfire for longer than a horse can think.

Sap knows nothing of horses, beyond the obvious — that their necks contain staircases that spiral to the stars. This one's is interrupted, however, by a shard of burning brass, a she-never-knew-what-hit-her shell fragment, all that remains of both blast and rider, the latter left behind, writhing in tall grass.

Hors. Hros. She runs what would be hands—were she distinct and outside the animal—all over its shudder-running mass, looking to comfort, cure, the what-is-it of the shell fragment, seething in the horse's own red. *Equus.* Hate hastens her, rage has rushed her into this state, this shape, plus her own heedless, riderless pain.

Cabbalus. Dreams can be realer than truth, but the irreality of seeing from either side of a head that was not hers somehow credited it—it was too improbable to be fantasy. *Hippos, ross.* How to settle on which side to see, which strand she clings to, or is it merely fists in mane?

She runs, the horse runs, it runs from front to front, covers ground recovered half a dozen times, rolling with poppies and kneaded with body parts, shredded webbing, steel. Clatter, bang; something big behind them, a line of men behind them, one man behind another behind them, and out in front, hedges and strange cuts in the soil, which is full, full of life that will witness their passage over it no more than a shadow of cloud. Gas. Yes. There's always that, to clear-kill everything: grass, grasshoppers, horse.

So it is when she stops in the railway cutting, between the German lines and their own advancing tide, that Sap, who has never seen John Herald in the flesh, guesses his importance by the way Stan speaks to him, as if talking a suicide off a ledge.

"That's not Blaze," he says, between gasps to rival all running with air. *Pumons, pumons. Briser.* Broken down, soldier-hearted. Men. The horse knickers as if it has seen it all. Sapphira almost grins. Then John says,

"It's her."

No, no, she shrieks from within the horse's skin, it's me—which is too much for the animal to bear. First, the

searing triangle, and now this. Sap's spirit body inside
the horse's actual, their senses skein into spirit bodies
running before and after, and trace the etymology of being,
becoming over earth in jussive hurls of hooves: *hors* outside
ros rose *ross* across *hros* heroes *hross* ghosts *aihwa* highway
equus equals *ippos* hippo *eoh*.

Ah. Ha ha! Ha, *Eoh*! *Hros*, ha!

77

TWELVE JOKERS

STAN'S PROBLEM wasn't determining which side were
they on (Allied or German; alive or dead), or, why were
they wearing gas masks underground (a not impossible
occurrence) when they clearly had something to hiss at him
("Sssstan ... Sssstan" got a little tiresome after a while). His
problem was being fixed to the floor on an upturned bayonet
made his heart skip beats like a stone over the pure pond of
his astonishment. He was three sheets to the windy when he
heard a very simple voice say, first, *Movement isn't everything.*
And then, *Since when were you interested in comfort?*

The figures surrounded him like hours on an excavated
sundial, twelve great-coated unter-beings all too clearly used to
being portentous and feared. He could never get a fix on them,
and even their helmets seemed to change back and forth, from
Tin Lizzies to *Stahlhelme* to something out of *Ivanhoe*. Only
the eyepieces of their respirators stayed the same, angling out
from either side of what had been a face, murky mirrors behind
which, presumably, were some kind of eyes.

The sense of Jenny above him, her strong presence on the
life side of the hole he'd fallen through, came and went, like
waking moments in a dream of sleep. And yet he was awake
and sleep itself seemed the capital enemy. Then he felt
them—not the goon squad—he felt the dead stir beneath
him, in caverns and grottos, subterranean reaches and ever-
dark beaches, washed up on the shores of identity, clinging
to memories, the flotsam and jetsam of some massive life
liner, the *Lusitania* of Lethe.

If these twelve jokers were anything, they were a link between those beneath and wherever Stan was, twelve feet under the road on which he and Jenny had been standing after the unveiling. Jenny had been taken with the goats, the ones that graze the grounds too thick with sleeping shells to mow. Stan had watched her watching them, and then lifted the hair from behind her ear—loving that little chute between lobe and neck, when the world went awry and Jenny jumped suddenly above him (so it seemed to Stan, falling) so that his first thought was she had been captured by heaven.

"Sssstan." It was the six o'clock goon, the one he saw directly at his feet. "Wee will ssshow you *awl*." Oh, please. "The pahssst, the few-tcher." How about a *moooving* picture? If it heard his mind, it made no sign. "Awl that roams beneath the mooon is ours. Sssstan."

If only they didn't lisp. Then, they really would have had him on. Whatever they had going on down there, beneath him, it wasn't the underworld, Achilles, or the missing of the Somme. It was more like an echo chamber, washed by sound-waves never dead.

"Give me back my friend," Stan managed (he didn't really know if he spoke or just thought out loud). It was a test.

"Ssssss." They shuffled and exchanged blank, mirror glances, each eyepiece flashing back to black. One of them started to laugh—do you have any idea what that sounds like behind a box respirator?—then stopped. The others looked at him. Looked away.

"My friend," Stan repeated, "I want to see my friend, John Herald," knowing more with each hiss he heard that these guys were … Jesus Christ they wailed like Jack Johnsons! The sound was almost more piercing than the bayonet, but it availed them nothing. Next thing you know, they're going to remove those masks.

"Show me some friends or show me your fucking faces."

For a moment, everything went dark. Then Stan was sitting up, nothing punctured, in the centre of the twelve, who sat cross-legged around him. Each one cradled something—Mausers, Lee Enfields, Lewis guns, the works. A few had Mills bombs in their hands; one had a pair of wire cutters; another, a flare pistol. Overall, they remained uniformly grey, or brown, or faintly blue, whichever it was—that patina of dried mud that plastered every crevice of their kit and clothing.

One gloved hand passed over the face of the first, and Sapphira's hair tumbled out from underneath the rubber mask. She was as she had been the day he joined the 108th Battalion in Toronto. She eyed him directly. "You'll have to ask mother," she said.

One gloved hand passed over the face of the second, and Jenny's starched veil unfolded about her head and shoulders like a stunsail. "Khaki greatcoat, cloak of blue, lie together—me with you," she recited the opening of the poem he wrote to her in Paris.

One gloved hand passed over the face of the third, and John Herald's blonde hair peeked out from under his officer's cap. How did he fit that in the mask? "I always came back," he said. And then, "*She* exists. *You* exist. If that weight is for you, if, together, you take on the ballast of being—you take that now."

One gloved hand passed over the face of the fourth. It was his mother, as he had left her in the asylum that day of the Corps Reunion in Toronto. "Better to rule in hell," she said, then, thinking better of it, "It's all right, Stan; your sister is dead."

One gloved hand passed over the face of the fifth. "You know why those three ampersands are there, boys?" the Colonel called out, over Stan's head and right through him at once. "They're the and, and, and that you are to me." Leading's voice shook the cavern so that little siftings of sand came down, as they used to during bombardments.

"You always do, you always have done, more than I ask. You're under an obligodamnation, now, to remember that."

One gloved hand passed over the face of the sixth, and out came Bill Ostic, his fetal head painted red with dried blood, tossing a Mills bomb from hand to hand. "What was that thing Herald had in his arms the night Fritz jumped us out beyond the wire?"

One gloved hand passed over the face of the seventh, and there was Art Cane, in mufti, answering, "Bill, every time you've had a few you ask me that, and every time I have the same answer for you: He didn't have anything in his arms, I don't know what you're talking about, ask Allward, he was there, too." Then, turning to Stan, added, "Hey, Mate."

One gloved hand passed over the face of the eighth, and—horses upon horses—it was a horse head, blazing like the harvest star through the grey mud that fell away from it like old paint. It said, nothing.

One gloved hand passed over the face of the ninth when ass ears flicked into view. It was the mule John had rescued from the quick mud of Passchendaele. It made a sound like an old hand pump outside the house.

One gloved hand passed over the face of the tenth, and Canon Scott's white collar showed up like a life raft in a sea of night. "I think you're painting your own signpost, son," and then, holding up a pale blue book, the Padre recited, "On lonely watches night by night, great visions burst upon my sight, for down the stretches of the sky, the hosts of dead go marching by."

One gloved hand passed over the face of the eleventh. It was his father. "Bricks and mortar, son; bricks and mortar for a city she's building in her mind."

"Will it take me in, Dad?" Stan wanted to ask, but wasn't at all convinced that any authentic piece of anything save the saccage of his own memory was being pulled out behind these gooney, face-sucking hat masks.

One gloved hand passed over the face of the twelfth. It was Stan himself:

"There are, essentially, three categories of people, three classes, three armies: the living, the wounded, and the dead. The living write histories. Sometimes, the wounded do. Well, after war, everyone is wounded. So that the borders between these three countries are not fixed. You will say, but the dead … but I repeat: the borders between these three countries (you must think of them all in one world, like three-thirds of a circle) are not fixed."

"I'll start again. On far end of the spectrum, you have the really alive. These are, generally, people before they join the army, but unfortunately, it also comes to include more and more soldiers and nurses, officers and batmen, the longer any of them survive—up to a point. Then they become wounded by default."

"I'll start again. The wounded, when they're *really* wounded—I don't know how else to say that, and mean nothing by it—i.e., when they're hit, cross over into a country that the un-hit living simply never know. It doesn't happen quickly, but before you are aware, it has happened, and there you are, shock-deep in pain, a denizen of vulnerability, and quite possibly death. At that point, if it wasn't already, everything becomes a charade. I don't mean false. I should have said show. Because now you must seem yourself, in order to be treated as yourself, which is your only chance. You'll never be unwounded, but you may be alive, again, if you're very, very careful."

"I haven't made my point. The point is that everything you describe in war, anything whatever you may say about it, is not war. War is not words, not even understanding. War is the process by which large numbers of the living become the wounded and the dead, against their wills and in the most violent ways imaginable. We hardly ever hear from those countries, or we hear from them all the time, because we are them. Our mistake, if we have one, is always to look at things from a living perspective. The championing of this point of view has lead to more nonsense being written than anything else in the world."

78

COMMUNION

THEY SMELLED THE HORSE before they could see it.
Country people. Churchgoers, their faces chevroned
above the vees of their upturned hymnals. Victory. The
choir had just processed by, and everybody was singing,
Holy, Holy, Holy, Lord God Almighty, underlined — as if for
emphasis — by the black hardback covers in their hands.

The doors remained open, on his hot summer day, and
John wondered if that mattered — he really was in the dark
about much of his non-being. He knew he could pick her
up; he knew he could lay her down. But he wasn't altogether
sure he and Blaze could walk through seasoned hardwood.
The world was still the world to him — world enough to
treat it as such. If it hadn't been, what would he be doing
here? What was he doing here?

> *Holy, holy, holy, Lord God Almighty,*
> *Early in the morning time, I lead my horse to thee.*

Again, unsure. Specifically, he was leading a horse to church,
the one that Fred Abercrombie attended — he was in there,
right now, singing to beat the devil. Victory. Over what?
Death? That death did not exist — was, in fact, a fiction — John
now knew. You can't defeat what isn't. And yet, he was himself
defeated. He could pick her up; he could lay her down; he
could throw her in the saddle and all three could leave the
ground. But. And in that hesitation lay all his undoing.

Lead my horse to water, let him drink; turn that water into wine. Make us real; help us stay a little longer.

Something along those lines was at work in the after-image of his mind. He was losing substance. More and more, when he touched her now, he felt it less and less. He was being withdrawn, and Blaze with him, horse and rider, abstract, beside her, their own little apocalypse in reverse: I will show you nothing. And so he felt, this former captain of scouts, this thief in the night of No Man's Land, that neither father, nor son, nor Holy Ghost could help him. No, it would have to be a farmer, someone used to failure, and that farmer would be Fred Abercrombie.

Blaze pawed at the door-sill and gave herself a shake. And then they walked right in. And everyone saw them, and no two saw anything different: John and Blaze, blonde and grey, uniformed and Fort Garry Horse, bandolier and cavalier, boots and spurs, cap and mane. They just walked right up the aisle and no one said a thing, until Blaze got up on the communion table, her hooves scrabbling the surface like a ship at sea, and turned as if to say goodbye. And then she simply, turned to dust.

79

TAKING FOREVER

"Jennabee?"

"Smallward?"

These are pet names you never hear; even I, who tell this story, have never heard them before.

"I don't want to go back to Toronto, again."

"Then don't!" she returns, crossly, tying the bandage as tight as she dare, hoping the gauze holds, that he doesn't breathe himself to death.

"We'll stay here," she adds, reassuringly, her bedside manner getting the better of her bitterness. "We can rent that ghastly little cottage in gruesome St. Julien and smoke ourselves breathless." I can't tie this tight enough, she thinks: the wound's inside. She could bind him to her breast and suckle him whole, but can't staunch what has no outlet.

"Sister Gray?" Stan gasps, with authority.

"Yes, Lieutenant."

"Take your time in dressing that wound."

"Don't you give orders to me!"

And then she realizes how far gone he is, how far, in fact, he has always been, and how close to something else she has seen far too often to mistake, now even in one she would blind herself with boiling pitch not to see, go.

"Jenny."

"Athel," she answers. "I'll take forever."

80

ASHES

SHE SLIDES ACROSS THE FLOOR to where Johnny sits in
the sun. He's fresh from the haying at Ed Abercrombie's.
His forearms are like furniture; she practically sits in his
lap. They fold into each other like thick toffee; the electric
hum of his hand on her spine enlarges the instant they are in.
Wherever they reach, there is always more; no need to forage
far afield: everything they want is right here, and no hurry to
get it in. Damp, and with the first drops of rain, her back.

Was there ever such a time? She wonders, peeling a strip
of paper curling from the heat of the kitchen wall. She
balls it in her fist, tosses it in the ash-can. This morning
she got up, to see his sleeping form coverless beside her.
Something's gone. She didn't know about the horse. She
reached out to touch his shoulder, *and her hand went right
through*. It was like mud, that reformed, the instant she
withdrew her fingers, into the wan constancy of a man she
would never know. She looked at her hand: ashen, ash-can;
whitish, pale glow — Whitsunday. He wasn't just returning
to wherever he came from — he was going back to *that*,
baptismal bone-yard chalk mud, the mud of the Somme, and
of the ridge at Vimy.

Ashes to ashes; dust to must. Get. Going. She couldn't
return, either, to school, or to church. Oh, fine — thank you;
I stopped fucking the ghost of John Herald. She would not be
the spirit whore of Carman. She just had to pick up and go.

John found her tossing whole drawers across the front
bedroom upstairs; eye-buckets of jewellery — old paste.

She saw Blaze standing behind her in the floor-length, oval mirror, and threw her mother's and her mother's and hers and hers and hers straight at it. Shattered, paste and wasted, false and true. Her inheritance of dusk from all those evenings alone.

"Emaiche ..."

"I was prepared for a lot of things, John Herald; I was prepared for you being not real; I was prepared for not being able to keep you if you were real; I was prepared for your real to mean there wasn't going to be any real left after you were gone — again, gone — along with every un- or fuck cunting real taken twice and heaved out the back of my heart like a shirt-waist worker afire. Burnt leavings. Sidewalk gods. I was pretty pre-fucking pared down to just about any possibility. But to see you go back to that blessed shit they call mud over there — it isn't mud, is it? It's *Saint Christos and His Travelling Ash-Can Circus*, isn't it? The same old bullshit at the well. And the clay he used to make them see. Mother Earth just isn't good enough for you boys. Too solid, pale rider. You have to atomize it into face powder for Mars; you will have absolution, but not at our hands. Buried in dirt, but married to your pasty-faced future-fucking family of ashen-eyed survivors. Save yourself, you blessed fucker. Wipe your own face, you concert-party cutout. You sure as sapphire can't save me from the loss of first earth, the actual arms of you, the loss of that. Go back to it, John Audet. Go back to your god of goo."

81

PALSIED

"AND IT CAME TO PASS on a certain day, as he was teaching, that there were Pharisees and doctors of the law sitting by, which were come out of every town in Galilee, and Judea, and Jerusalem: and the power of the Lord was present to heal them." Church parade. The Colonel reads the text of the service from a lectern supported by two empty bomb boxes, two brassy snare drums. Around him, in an open (that is, three-sided) square, stands the entire complement of the 108th Battalion, some thousand men, in the last summer of the war.

"And behold, men brought in a bed a man which was taken with a palsy: and they sought means to bring him in, and to lay him before him." Leading looked up at his men. Church parade is not about belief, anymore. The men have worked out their trench religion, complete with talisman's, do's and don'ts, luck, and fate. It includes Christ—sacrificially one of them—but not his church. Leading knows this. He just wants to tell them a story.

"And when they could not find by what way they might bring him in because of the multitude, they went upon the housetop, and let him down through the tiling with his couch in the midst before Jesus."

He paused, looked up. Paused. "A stretcher case, surely," he added, and an underlaugh rippled through the ranks and files. Beloved. My God, he said to himself, I can hardly take them all, at once; my dear God, he repeated, let me lead them well.

"And when he saw their faith, he said unto him, Man, thy sins are forgiven thee." When a member of the battalion was killed, the duty of reviewing the man's crime sheet fell to the Colonel. It would be sent on to his next of kin. And Leading, with possibly his adjutant and certainly the battalion diarist within earshot, would look at the — quite possibly long — list of defaults and infringements of military life (a missing this, a messing up that; sometimes, missing altogether), and pronounce, "This man had no crimes." He would then tear up the sheet — a sound that he both loved to make and hated to hear — have one of his staff draw up a pristine replacement, and write (when time permitted) a sincere letter of condolement. Scribal justice.

"And the scribes and the Pharisees began to reason, saying, Who is this which speaketh blasphemies? Who can forgive sins, but God alone?"

"What I want to know, at this point, boyos," he said, letting his monocle fall and hit the page from which he read, "is two things: one, what is this sick fellow thinking at this time? Did he really go to all that trouble of getting his friends to bust through the roof and winch him over like a piece of field ordnance to hear that he was jake with the man upstairs? And second, if he didn't, then what in Jack Christ is sweet Jesus up to?" (You can't take the Lord's name in vain if you address him in the same breath, Leading reasoned in his heart.)

"He must know that's not what the palsied man wants. Surely it must be obvious at this point in the life of our Lord that when sappers dismantle a rooftop to lower a stretcher case in front of him, that the bugger wants to *walk*, damn you, not become Exhibit A in theological parley over who can forgive whom. Why does he answer good faith with bad? But I'll go on."

The officers at least feign attention, but they can see their charges starting to sway into stand-up sleep. Men learned to do that, during the war — leaning against a trench wall. Stan has yet to see an entire battalion sleep free-standing. Maybe this will be the day.

"But when Jesus perceived their thoughts, he answering said unto them, What reason ye in your hearts? Whether it is easier, to say, Thy sins be forgiven thee, or to say, Rise up, and walk?" Leading paused again. For almost a minute — a silence which, oddly enough, woke up every man in the unit. It's harder to not be able to say, Rise up.

❈

Stan cannot. Rise up, that is, at all. The bayonet has him fixed like an exotic, rare butterfly in a dungeon of curiosities. Jenny kneels beside him, thinking hard. They can lower a stretcher, and haul it up again — but how to get Stan on it?

Then she knows. They have to reconstitute the stretcher, which she is already splitting down the middle with Stan's pocket knife, beneath Stan, between him and the earth, without lifting him, and then uses the four ropes to pull him straight off the blade.

Which means she needs help, here below. Ostic, Cane, and someone Stan doesn't recognize, shimmy down the two ropes with which they had lowered Jenny, one beneath each shoulder, into the pit itself — which stunk, I should add, something awful: old gas, old gas blankets, old khaki, old sweat. Powder. Old gunpowder. Rotten eggs.

Stan has stopped speaking; Jennie whimpers as she works; Bill and Art pretend not to hear. Who's that other one? Stan wonders. His vision is going, everything is going away home, when the one he was wondering about appears, suddenly, above him.

"Which is easier," he asks, "to say your sins are forgiven you, or to haul you off that blade alive?" Good question, Stan thinks.

"Dear one"—it's Jenny, now—"this is going to hurt, I'm afraid."

"Don't be afraid," the fifth says to Stan, who seems to be the only one who can hear him.

"Is it really like you say it is?" Stan asks.

"Well, I don't know about the *really*, but I'm all over like. Very *like* a whale, my son; lamps go out of his mouth continually."

"He is king over all the children of pride," Stan recites, wanting to perform and impress, even now.

"Who are you talking to, Mate?" Art asks.

Jenny thinks he's delirious. He is. But oddly, it's Ostic who figures it out. "He's all right, Sister."

"William," Jenny says, unable to bear it. And because she calls him that, and the way he says it, Stan thinks Bill thinks he (Stan) has just learned what he already knows. He puts a hand on Bill's strong one.

"We all had to share," he whispers. He's talking about Ward nurses in Stationary Hospitals. Bill knew he knew, but thought Stan was pretending he didn't. Stan still wants to know if he was seen seeing, and if so—does Jenny know he saw? He doesn't want her to live with that, with him gone. Not the fact of it—she looked, in fact, quite good on her back in the gothic company of moony headstones—just that he saw. Now, with the stretcher reconstructed complete underneath him, there's some hesitation over the actual hauling that breaks—

"Lift me up," Stan commands.

"It might kill you."

But Stan no longer believes in death. "Lift me up; lift me up," he repeats. A jolt, as four other pilgrims, hastily recruited as haulers up above, heave-ho together. He's heavy enough; the bayonet makes the work even harder. Stan screams as the blade exits his body on the rise. Jenny's hands slip away from his forearm as up he goes. By the time the setting sun of Vimy hits his eyes, he is very, very light.

❋

"But that ye may know that the Son of man hath power on the earth to forgive sins, he said unto the sick of the palsy, I say unto thee, Arise, and take up thy couch, and go into thine house."

Leading looks up; starts to speak, when —

"*And this time use the front door, for Chrissakes!*" cat-called from the ranks.

"There ends the lesson," the Colonel said. The Typos cheered him deaf.

82

REMOUNT

"You've lost your horse," Fred said, matter-of-factly, aware that any show of pity would only humble John more than either man could bear. Killing, in war, is like that: humbling someone more than either man — or beast — can bear, and so finishing them off, if they aren't dead already.

Moral force, John remembered. He remembered someone saying, after he was gone but before he came back (there's a fault there, somewhere) that as long as moral force prevails, war will always imply war to the bitter end. Maybe that's what brought him back, that bitter end, the outrageous outrage of morality. He stood there, far beyond the end of his tether, and fixed Fred with blue eyes already transparent with the light behind them, and said,

"Any chance of a remount?"

And Fred laughed his enormous laugh.

83

DREADFUL REASON

WHAT A *dreadful* reason to be here, he thought. Stan surprised himself with that, stretching his legs beyond St. Julien, leaving its stone-staring soldier far behind. How far? Oh, I'd say a good fifty metres. It didn't take much. To leave the war behind, I mean. A shrug of muggy straps, a falling off from sweat-stained backs, rifles stacked, the S-clasps of their belts undone, unwinding their puttees: a forestful of serpents down two hundred thousand trees. Caducous.

"What a *dreadful* reason to be here. What a *dreadful* reason." She was mocking him, walking beside him, her bare feet (now, that was new) sudden in the dun dawn, fields a little streaming with the dew.

"Well, it is."

"How is that, Piperoo?" She meant the "pips," or diamond-shaped studs that had marked him as an officer—mouldering, now, at home. "You haven't known this place any other way. How is that your fault?"

"*That's* a different question."

"It's the same question, put *differently*."

The road glistened a wet charcoal gray; poppies daubed the multi-green margins like scarlet cream.

"There is going to be another."

"Yes."

"We didn't finish, here; we weren't allowed."

"No."

"Will it be worse than the first one?"

"That, again, will not be your fault."

My, my, but haven't we grown up, Stan thought. Then he looked at her, and she wasn't just thin—she was a wisp of a wisp, her plaster-of-Paris skin stretched wan on a frame of angry bones. She wore right through whatever she wore, which was next to nothing. Somewhere in those sockets, Sapphira's eyes were fixed on a future that would abolish time altogether.

Part of Stan, he knew, was running back up the road, back to his shell-shocked assurances that the worst was past. But he surprised himself a second time, that morning on the far side of the world, by stopping and then steering her far shoulder towards him with one finger-shroud like a sail.

"Wait," he said, and bent down, gathered little purple eyelets together with the red-eyed mouths, and made of them a bomb-sized bouquet.

"A spray for the spook," he said, smiling straight into the horror of her. She cupped them in her fingers' pale; teeth grown rotten bared a grateful glare.

"Shall these bones live?" she asked him, truly, asking, him: as if it were his decision.

Stan followed his feet beside hers along the margin of the road. She had no room among the living, or the dead; nowhere to rest her over-weary, Medusa head.

"Yes, Sapster," he said. "I do think they will."

And she didn't disappear, for the longest time.

84

MARRY ME

EVERY EVENING, it's the same, damn scene: apologetic, quiet men gather at the back of the Abercrombie home in Carman—where Fred grew up and where his father, Ed, still lives—and wait for what they neither have the right to ask for nor their hosts to refuse. Difficult to tell, at this distance, how, exactly, the dirty thirties got their moniker. But if you saw these men, up close, you would not be in doubt for long. There is no question of them coming inside the house, although a storm might see them into the barn or some other outbuilding. Mrs. Edward eventually appears, with help—local girls in need of home economy—and out comes the old crockery, the chipped sets, the ruined cutlery, and soup—blessed soup—and bread, and sometimes vegetables, cigarettes—even coffee.

This evening, Fred is the help. His mother has cancer; she is not doing well. And her slow son needs to keep his quick hands occupied, his mind distracted. He wants Mary Helen. For the first time in his life—ever since the dance—he just wants her. No love, no charity. This is far harder than it sounds. It's not a question of finding a quiet corner with a sly magazine—there are no quiet corners, and certainly no magazines for Fred Abercrombie. I could say, his sexuality was like the weather, but what would that do for you? The weather is not like the weather anymore than a bombardment is like a firecracker in a frog's mouth. Fred was in heat, and it was hot; he was in need, and there was nought.

How had he hedged it until now? Love of the land? Call it absorption. When every aspect of your world is alive for you and to you, not because it's beautiful or you are so inclined but because everything—the day, the light, the time, the month, the weather, the year, the person, the help, the cattle, the moon, the incremental changes of all goring things (that's a typo, but I'm keeping it)—touches on your immediate, material well-being, well, it takes something of a fanatic to cry, *This* sensation, and no other, is what I seek. The world is not prophylactic, it teems and for once, Fred Abercrombie was dead to the world. Spending time with these guys just seemed natural.

We are the dead. Short years ago, they lived, felt dawn, saw sunset grow into a night that swallowed nations. It was never meant to come to this: Mary Helen in love with a ghost; Christ proved a liar; his own reticent, glad-but-not-handing, open, robust, shrewd, protectionist gallantry, so long maintained, in all weathers—kicked away, of its own rootlessness, like a tumbleweed of parasols tangled up and blown away by someone or some thing that did not even exist—let alone her own desire, to have that or nothing, and to settle for nothing over him.

Bread and bowls for filthy hands: the cracked one, those three, pale, green lines before the chip; that man's thumbnail clear gone. Their pink fingertips, which they suck clean before touching anything, as if wearing stunted gloves of dirt, and then, what clean fingers and what pale hands were—held his calloused hands up in—these? Mary Helen. Her and no John.

"Not to worry, Frederick" (pressing his together, now, in prayer between both of hers): "Marry me."

85

HERO

"I DON'T HATE HEROICS," Stan said. "I'd just like to know what they are."

Jenny does not ask, "Didn't the war beat that out of you?" She's done the arithmetic. She knows that, as for trauma, she and Athelstan are neck and neck. But she didn't know front-line service. She didn't know that ... thing ... that men thought they reserved for themselves alone. Raising your head above the parapet, facing the faceless face of war.

"They start with you and me," she says instead, surprising even herself. "And they don't end until time ends us. I remember when I first saw you—"

"You first saw my ass. You didn't see me at all."

Face down in assless shit, Jenny thought, laughing. Shrapnel in his gluteal cleft. She knew him intimately long before she knew the first thing about him.

"I knew you ... intimately," she says, measuring out her own thought, "long before I knew the first thing about you."

Stan stops brooding over his sense of injured shame. He wants to know.

"I knew you were a hero, Stan. What do you suppose brought me here in the first place?" First place, first things. "A stationary hospital in France in 1917 is nowhere to go looking for cowards. I knew you were a hero because you came to me broken. That was done before you first laid eyes on me. Who did that to you? And it seemed to me that I spent a long time cradling you in my thoughts. I didn't give myself to you—"

The café in Mons was almost empty. Most everyone connected with the pilgrimage had left for home. There were always veterans, of course; and Stan seemed strangely contemporary with the war that was, because of the armful of bandages wrapped around his chest. Almost hit his heart, that bayonet.

"... because you were brave or because you were kind or because of the poems you wrote on the stationery I stole for you or the way you waited, patient, immobile, ranked with your mates in the Nova Scotia Ward. I gave myself to you because ..." and here she, indescribably, trailed off.

"Because I asked you?" Stan hazarded. Maybe if he spoke the truth. It wasn't just that she slept, sort of, with the best Lewis-gunner in the battalion — a man haunted by a period ad for a hair tonic that did not work. If he knew about Lo, possibly he would not have felt as grateful as he did for these words of hers. Athelstan Allward was a modern man, but he wasn't Superman.

"I don't recall you asking," she said, coyly, then resumed. "No, dear; I gave myself because you were wide open to receive what I had on offer. And when you give like that, there are no takers." She let him take that in. His bandages seeped a little.

"I gave myself to you because you were broken in your bravity." She paused on the word, arcane and distant, compliment and critiscm, and so like brevity, then softened, but only a little.

"And I gave myself because you are the hero of my heart," she added, conceding a piece of her immense regard for him. He had, after all, gone over, AND MORE THAN ONCE, she saw, inscribed on a tombstone in her mind:

THIS STONE MARKS THE
HEART OF ONE JENNABETH
GRAY WHO GAVE HERSELF
AWAY TO A SOLDIER THE 23RD
APRIL OF THE GREAT, GREAT
1917 THOUSANDS LIE ABOUT
LOVE THERE IS NONE NEARBY

"And because you had a gluteal cleft like the wake of the *Titanic*."

She knocked back her whisky.

"*Garson*," Stan called, *à la* Bill, "the same, again, please."

She took his hand.

86

SWEETHEART

I THOUGHT THIS ROCK face would never end, Stan had thought, but it did, and, almost as suddenly, as if waking from a bad dream, they were in a flat world of scrub pine, and then mature meadow, and then, after a time—and vastly—field after field after field. No tenders therein. There seemed to be no end to it: wholly the sky spanned above them, even in front of them, as if they were already beyond the horizon.

And now, John Herald does a curious thing. He pulls the shell fragment from Blaze's neck, just as you might take a pocket handkerchief from a jacket, and throws it away like a thing of another time. He pats her neck where there is now, no wound—Stan thinks, inevitably, of the last spade flat on a grave—and then arcs himself high into the saddle, a pasteboard sun worked by offstage flies as quick as blinking.

"I'd ask you to ride with me, but ..." Herald trails off, looking down at Stan and then away. Stan can't tell whether he's smiling or not.

"It's good to see you."

"You, too."

"You know, I went back to find my sweetheart."

"You never told me you had a sweetheart!"

"Well, I did, but I didn't want you to be jealous," John said, for effect—Stan got it, saw that, caught it with a sleight-of-eye from his flickering face—"and I couldn't write ... to her ... couldn't write for shit, actually, which you kind of knew."

"How ever did you get your commission?"

"Battlefield promotion. Seconded from the angles and jags, again and again. No one read the ground like me. You knew that. Besides, you've always known," John adds, only now he seems to be talking about something else.

"Anyway, I had a sweetheart. Her name was Mary Helen. I can't take her with me."

"Why not?"

"Because there has been someone else with me, all the time."

"You mean Blaze?" John shakes his head, and stares at his friend for what seems a very long time, whatever time means, in that world.

"This is not my dream, old campaigner. Think back, to Amiens," he says, "to what you saw, in the trench, at Amiens," he goes on, "after I was gone." And John smiles his faraway smile.

Sapphira comes out from behind Blaze like a star around the moon.

"Is the horse me?" she asks, super-naturally-cilious.

"Sap!"

"What took you so long?"

GO

H<small>E WAS THERE</small>, all right, and such readiness in his manner, such longing in his eyes, as if he could be torn in two ways about her. Was she, was she ... where was she? And he scanned and he scanned and he scanned. What was that white one, in the door, apsed by a halo of hair, off-white from head to foot in ... nude. She came down the aisle, naked as the day she was, and was covered — her skin, all uncovered — in ashes.

My stars but his eyes fell! You could hear them as they hit the. And then, there were so many things to disarrange: the after-service gatherings and teas, all lost. She was lost to him for so, so long ago.

Frederick Snelgrove Abercrombie, you were meant for leaner joys than this, momentary palimpsest: you trace her line of vantage from the crease of thighs and rise and rise again. Release. Her. Release.

YOU CAN EAT ANYTHING

"It's too early for coffee," Lois says. She holds a gin and orange juice in one hand and a cup of coffee in the other. "You can eat *anything* at breakfast," she adds, staring at Jenny through a haze of cigarette smoke. "You just burn it up."

Jenny pulls her limbs in from the scattered outposts of the bed—a four-poster, in fact, with an eagle hanging over her, hewn out of the headboard. "That's food for you." Jenny pauses, takes the mug, stares at her own words in space. Why did everything multiply its meanings in Lois's presence? She sees the blue notebook in her hands. "So, you found it."

"Yes. I'm sorry. I went through your luggage. Couldn't wait. Did you ... of course, you never met her."

"In a way," Jenny says, and cups her hands and hair over the steaming mug. "In a way, you can't miss her, I mean, because he does, so much. I've given up trying to replace her. So I became her archivist."

"What did you archive?"

"Oh, anything, everything, I guess. Mobiles, mainly; shapes, odd drawings—I mean drawings she did with John Odd, Junior ... and notebooks. It's in code."

"No kidding."

"Can you make it out?"

"Well, she was a secretive little girl, and no mistake, but she did supply an alphabet on the back page, so she wasn't very good at it."

"How do you know it's the right one?"

"Because I've been spending all morning deciphering the first page."

"What does it say?"

> This city is my mind to me
>   ever since you went away;
>   this city is a blind to be
>   drawn against the day

"It's poetry?"

"You bet," Lo says, and almost smacks her lips on the last of the orange juice. "Written straight across. Like the Greeks," she adds, "like Sappho."

"Sapphira."

"She was some little woman."

"Keep on going," Jenny urges, sitting up now, her head clearing. Lo puts her cigarette out in the dregs of her glass, and begins:

89

POSSIBLE

MORNING CAME. He would not go. Noontime brought the supper on. He stayed. She hoped and wept and prayed. Go. Don't go. Don't. Go. He turned the matter over in his mind. What is eternal, now? Had he missed a step? Was he the only one? Or was he nobody, once his body was no more? Could not distinguish between sleep and waking, between the train station in Carman and a ship at sea. Memory of her. Was all this his memory of her, concocted, thrown backwards in time while he died on the wire?

That would mean an actual her. That would mean to be unbearable. And why? Because you can't ride it. It rides you, bullet-ridden, and her impossibly gone. It is possible, possible, possible. It must be. John Herald walked and stirred; his hair wound into Prairie wheat, his ears prick the fields. Possible.

Enter Stan, following him and Blaze — which we know, Stan said in his mind, actually happened. It didn't surprise him — well all right it surprised him, mildly, to see Stan show up before he died. The Canadian Shield. That took twenty years, to cross back home.

He comes from the tall grass, buffalo, last of ten thousand, and sees her hair weaving the wind like sere. He takes her hand. Kisses her mouth. I was never here, my dear; I was never here. She starts to speak, and the bullets fly straight from her.

90

SAP RISING

SHE WAKES, as she always wakes, to the smell of yeast. Hair-snarled head breaches from bleached sheets, dun feet kick away the leavenings of night. Sap rises to the city she loves, its stove-pipe streets newly sheathed in black macadam, its sidewalks still wooden slats, and her two eyes—twin ribbons of vision—railing them silver, shuttering perspective to the edge of sight. Shuttering, fluttering, her brother in the room beside hers, muttering, *Get up, Sapphira; the dough has been kneaded, the ovens fired; the first loaves have long been ladled in.*

How can Stan stand to miss this? Yeast and yearning and purple-dawn streets? Yeast and—if she were ever away from it long enough to notice—coal, its black dust sifting from chimneys, filling the hour-glass of industry: back alley factories, carriage and piano works, forgings, tanneries, and lumber-yards, carpet-makers and ironmongers—and not least the bakery itself, a mere whiff away. She hears its horses stamp and toss. Iron rims rumble on cobblestones in the yard. She drew these sounds long before she knew what they were—vast yeast beasts, floating on thunder, sailed onto Sullivan Street, her home. A street of new Canadians from the old world: English workers in two-storey row housing on the north side; their foremen and artisans in the three-storey row south.

Slam door, look round, button-up boot-soles spring from porch boards: a girl takes to the sidewalk as an otter to water: Sapphira Allward, twelve years old in the Toronto of 1914. Amber hair, amber eyes, ambling along, she.